THE BREACH HOUSE ANTHOLOGY

THE BREACH HOUSE ANTHOLOGY

Stories, Poems, Essays, Memories

Edited by Edward Lemond and Lee D. Thompson

Breachhousebooks
Barachois, New Brunswick

Lemond, Edward and
Thompson, Lee D.

The Breach House Anthology

ISBN: 978-0-9737628-4-6

First paperback edition 2010

Breachhousebooks
Chemin de la Brèche
Barachois, NB

CONTENTS

FOREWORD

The Breach House Gang

I am a visual artist and words play a prominent role in my art. In 1997 I began to write poetry in my studio at the Aberdeen Cultural Center in Moncton, New Brunswick. As writing took on greater importance in my work, I suggested to my friend and artist Nancy Morin that we get together to read and critique our poetry. These sessions were so motivating that I began to look for other writers who might also be searching for this type of activity. I heard about a second hand book store located downtown called The Attic Owl where owner and writer Ed Lemond and his wife Elaine Amyot (writer and painter) held lively meetings for artists to get together one evening each month. Invited writers and visual artists from Moncton and the surrounding area provided a diverse program in exchange for enthusiastic audiences that filled all available chairs and lined the stairs. It was a privilege to attend these meetings and to meet others with similar interests.

In 1999 when my studio (the Breach House) was completed in Grand Barachois, I decided to open it to writers and invited Ed Lemond and Elaine Amyot, Nancy Morin and Lee Thompson to form a group. This was the beginning of the Breach House Gang and eventually other Attic Owl participants Elizabeth Blanchard, Beth McLaughlin, Noeline Bridge and Anne Lévesque accepted to make the drive to Grand Barachois on a Sunday each month. A recent member, Acadian visual artist and writer Roméo Savoie of Grand Barachois, joined the gang in 2008.

We have a very simple way of operating. Each person brings something to read, and then we talk about what we've just heard. We offer words of encouragement and, where it seems called for, words of criticism. Our aim is always to help the writer see what's good in the material and what could be further developed and brought to life. We have survived for ten years for one simple reason: we like one another's company and we always come away from our meetings on a high, even when we know there's much work still to be done.

Nancy King Schofield
Chemin de la Brèche
Grand Barachois, New Brunswick

Frozen Pears, Nancy King Schofield, 2009

Anne R. Lévesque

GOING TO MARRY JESUS

Left, then right, then towards her empty wine glass, Jessie is sweeping bread crumbs on the tablecloth. I hear the soft crushing sound they make as they roll on the cloth. I watch her brown silver-ringed hand in the candlelight.

We have had our mother's strawberry shortcake, our tea with canned milk and then more wine, and this lull in the conversation would be a good time to clear the table, wash the dishes, lift sleeping children from bedrooms to cars and other houses.

Yet we stay.

Elbows on the table, we lean towards each other, away from the shadowy edges of the room, from yet another separation.

For like all families, our history is one of separations.

We had been talking about trains. How you had to drive all the way to Truro to take the train now. How the old station was going to be turned into a museum.

"The first time I took the train, it was from the station in Kenloch."

My mother's head tilts up. She looks at me in that sharp way she used to have when she'd caught me out in a lie.

"Kenloch! Are you that old, John?" Linda says.

My sisters laugh, smug in the knowledge that no matter how old they become I will always be older.

But then they are quiet.

I remember that morning, sitting between my grandfather and my mother in his Dodge pick-up, a soft wrinkled paper bag of Yellow Transparents in my lap. I couldn't see much out the window so I looked at my grandfather as he drove. The road to the train station was one that he rarely traveled so he was looking around with curiosity.

"Now look at that," he snorted. "Left their hay rotting in the fields."

And then: "It's a clear mystery to me why people would start building a house and just abandon it."

"Maybe they changed their minds." my mother said. "Maybe something happened." But he had not answered.

In the back of the truck was a dark-green trunk with brass fittings. The day before I had watched my mother and her sister kneeling beside it on the painted wooden floorboards of my mother's room. Someone had spread a sheet over the bed and piles of carefully folded clothing lay on top of it. My best clothes were going in the trunk. My second-best I was to wear on the train; the rest was staying behind.

"You won't be needing those now, Johnny. You'll be a city boy." my mother said.

"A city boy," Aunt Mary echoed, "wearing fancy clothes and walking on sidewalks."

The prospect of wearing my good clothes did little to cheer me. I had a bad feeling about this move. My mother had only said that we were moving to Toronto and that I was to have a daddy now, Joseph MacLellan. Until then I had not known that I did not have a daddy. I knew Joseph MacLellan, though. He had visited my mother often that summer. A small quick man with bright blue eyes, he smoked cigarettes and did not pay much attention to me. If he was going to be my daddy, I could not see how that would be any improvement over my present situation.

Aunt Mary had cried when she kissed me goodbye that night, and so had my grandmother and mother as they embraced the next morning. This did nothing to alleviate my fears. But the prospect of traveling on a train with my mother was so exciting that my apprehension was soon replaced by anticipation.

"That was *my* first time on the train too," my mother says. "Twenty-three years old and I had never been farther than Port Hood! Imagine that." Her hazel eyes are bright in the candle light. It's a quality I have only noticed recently. When I mentioned it to her she laughed:

"Do they still shine, then? People often used to tell me that."

"Of course women didn't travel as much then; oh, they went to the Boston States to become servants, but that was about it. When I boarded the train there was only one other woman in our compartment. She waited until I had found a seat and then she asked if she could sit with us. She was a big girl, shoulders as wide as a man and big husky brown hands. Looked like she had pitched hay all summer. She told me she was going to Montreal, to become a Carmelite nun.

"She waved at her family through the window. Her mother was crying, her little brother was crying, and after the train pulled away from the station she cried too, poor thing. I felt sorry for her. And then I thought; we're kind of in the same boat. I was going away to marry Joe MacLellan, she was going to marry Jesus.

"Now you know how it is when you're traveling, as soon as you're off, you're hungry. I don't know why, but that's how I am, anyway. Even if I'm just going to Sydney. I guess it's the boredom. Or the excitement, I don't know. Well, not twenty minutes after the train left the station she took out a box and set it on her lap. She was right next to me so when she opened it I saw that it was her lunch. And right there on top of the sandwiches, there was a letter. She read it right away. Then she folded it and put it in the pocket of her dress. She didn't say a single word to me after this.

"When we got to Port Hastings she took her lunch and her little bag and coat and left. Didn't take the ferry. Didn't board the train for Montreal. Not that day, anyway. Just up and left.

"I've often wondered what was in that letter to make her change her mind like that. Something to do with a man, I figure. I've thought about her often over the years. I never found out who she was. I asked around but no-one knew of her.

My mother stops to light a cigarette. Her head bent towards the flame, she looks up at us, smiles as if to say Who wants to hear this old story again, anyway?

But I've never heard the story of the Carmelite nun. And I would wager that my sisters have not heard it too. My mother has always been rooted in the present. And she was too busy to tell stories. She left that to my step-father.

I don't remember the girl, nor do I remember taking the ferry and the other train. But I remember the lunch my grandmother had prepared. There were biscuits wrapped in paper and a crumbly piece of white home-made cheese, her thick molasses cookies. The biscuits had been spread with the dark yellow butter that my mother churned once a week, from the cream that cultured behind the woodstove. I have never forgotten the smell of that kitchen when I came down the stairs in the morning. The sharpness of milk souring for cheese, the smoke that escaped from the stove lids whenever someone threw in a chunk of wood, the smell of manure, from my grandmother's barn clothes in the entrance. For she would have already milked the cows then, would be putting milk through the separator or washing its many parts. She was always the first one up.

At the next stop, a fat woman boarded the train with a girl about my age. The man across the aisle offered them his seat and asked my mother if he could sit with us. My mother moved closer to the window and he sat next to the aisle. I was in between them so I had to crane my neck to look at the newcomers. I was interested in the girl, who was the only other child on the train, but she avoided my eyes. I watched them taking off their coats, hanging them up, moving their bags, taking them out to rummage through them, putting them away again, until I fell asleep in the clanking, swaying coach.

When I woke up, the air in the train was thick with the smell of sandwiches and dirty socks and blue with cigarette smoke. I was thirsty.

For the first time, I took a good look at the man who had come to sit beside me. He had a round flat face and a wide nose. The back of his big hands was covered with black hair and he seemed foreign and repulsive to me. I sidled towards the window and my mother, only to discover that she was gone. She was waiting in line for the lavatory at the other end of the rail car and came rushing back when she heard me. She chided me for being such a sooky baby, apologized to the stranger and moved me beside the window. That's when she noticed that I had wet myself. "Johnny!" she said. As my clothes were all in the green trunk, there was nothing to do but wait. The little girl looked at me with interest now.

I dared not move for a long time. I watched the trees and fields and houses going by. I listened to the men behind us talking about the mining job they were going to. I looked at our new seatmate again. Now that my mother had separated us, he turned out not to be so frightening. He had wavy black hair combed back and parted on the side, and like most men then his face was sun-burned. My mother was turned towards him and they were talking. They spoke softly so I could not catch their words.

When the train stopped in Moncton, the man invited us for supper in the dining car. We followed him down the now still train. There was one heavy door after another to push open and many thresholds to cross.

I had never eaten in a restaurant before. I remember the silverware and glass on the white tablecloth, the waiter, who was the first black man I had ever seen, and as night fell, my mother's reflection in the window; her flowing brown hair and freckled thin face and resolute mouth. I used to think that her poise and self-confidence had been gained through experience and age, but I now know that she had always been strong-willed and straight, unwavering in her opinions. She had not given me up at a time when girls in her situation went away to have their babies and put them up for adoption, or hastily married the fathers.

Many years later, at another table, my sisters and I listen to her.

"I had never met Neil but I knew his people. So he wasn't a complete stranger. He was going to Sudbury to work in the mines. We discovered that we had a lot in common. Neither one of us wanted to leave Cape Breton, for one thing. I don't think we slept that night; we just talked and talked.

"He didn't waste any time; that was never his way. He told me that come springtime, he was moving back to Cape Breton to the farm that he had inherited from his great-uncle. It was far from the village but there were neighbours, and many acres of cleared fields and a good house and barn. It didn't have the electricity yet, but that was bound to come. There was gravity-fed water and plenty of maple and birch to burn; he thought that he could make a living there.

"He said that if I could wait until the spring we would get married and go live there and I wouldn't have to go live in a city, away from my family. He wanted to marry me right away, that day.

"Well, I didn't know what to think. It wasn't that I had fallen in love with him, but that I knew that I could. Easily. And if I could fall in love with the first stranger I met on a train, what was I doing getting married to Joe MacLellan? I realized what a fool I had been. Thinking that he was the best I could hope for."

The train station in Montreal was bigger than I had imagined a building could be, with ceilings higher than any barn or church. There were more people there than I had ever seen together before, people walking in every direction, and fast. My mother had to do something about our tickets so we spent some time waiting in line. Then she said that she had to send a telegram and we stood in another line. After that we sat on a bench in that great busy hall. My mother was silent. I could sense that something was wrong. After a few minutes Neil Beaton arrived. He seemed very tall and dark as he stood in front of us.

My mother looked up and said: "It's done."

And then she began to cry.

"So we went to Sudbury. Just like that. I'm still amazed at this. It's like another person made that decision, not me. And maybe it was. Maybe it was Neil. It was hard to say no to Neil.

"I stayed with Willie and Jesslyn. Willie and Neil knew each other. They had worked together at Falconbridge Mine. I got a job in a doctor's house. Doctor Malcom Ferrin. He was a good man but his wife was hard to work for. John stayed home with Jesslyn. She was expecting and he was a great help with Colin, who had just started to walk.

"In the spring, Neil and John and I took the train back home and we were married two weeks later."

My mother stubs out her cigarette.

"And that was it," she says. "I never got on a train again."

Neil Beaton did, however.

13

He left for the mines the year after Theresa was born. My mother has said that they needed the money. But there are always other reasons for leaving. Maybe he felt hemmed in on the farm, with a wife and two small children. Or maybe he missed the camaraderie of working men. The freedom. The road.

When I think of that winter, I see my mother lighting the kerosene lamp on the table after the sun went down, and how peaceful it was in the house, just me and her and the baby.

I didn't go to school while Neil was gone. I fed the chickens, brought in firewood, shoveled a path to the outhouse. Twice a day she would put Theresa in the sleigh under a big blanket and I would pull her round and round the house and barn while she milked the cow and did the chores.

In the spring, my grandfather drove to the train station in Kenloch to pick up Neil's coffin. He had been killed by a rock fall in Sudbury.

I imagine Neil Beaton sitting at the table with us. His skin smooth, his blue eyes clear, spared the failings and losses that come with age. That come with living. And then I see them all: The nineteen-year old who fathered me, whose features I have memorized from an old school photograph I cut out in the newspaper. He died in a car accident when I was thirteen. And Andy Donnelly the story-teller, the card-player and drinker, with whom my mother had two more daughters. Gone now too. All the fathers of my mother's children.

Now and at the Hour

Forgive those who trespass against us lead us not into temptation but deliver us from evil for thine is the kingdom and the power and the glory for ever and ever amen. Just my luck Willy had to be in Halifax, getting some tests at the VG; Doctor Lauchie says it's nothing but Willy was worried, I could tell. Men are such sooks about doctors. Colin wouldn't go near one, he said if something was wrong he'd rather not know. But then look what happened to him. Look what happened to me.

You're healthier than the rest of us put together, I said to Willy. I think it made him feel better. What I didn't say was how surprising that is, with all the smoking and drinking and carrying on that man's done. Poor Nettie. Spent all those years dragging him home from the Legion and getting him to the detox when he was too far gone. And now that she's dead he's as sober as a judge. There's no justice in the world, that's what I say. But that Willy's no fool; with Nettie gone he knew he'd be dead in a year if he didn't stop drinking.

I was happy when he moved into the units, though. Right next doors, too; men are so scarce around here that's like winning the 649. I made some oatcakes and brought him over a big plate. Knew I'd get him that way, knew he'd be missing Nettie's baking.

I love feeding a man. Women just pick and judge. They're saying those are the best lemon squares they ever ate, what's the recipe, and when you tell them they say; Oh. No wonder it's good. All that butter. As if you cheated or something.

Doctor Lauchie's after me about the butter too, and the salt. Dawn says I'm the apple type. She saw it on Oprah. It's supposed to mean I'll have heart problems, I should watch what I eat, start walking more. I'd like to see how far she could go with this cane. She's built just like me, that's what she's worrying about. Always dieting and going to the gym and then she'll come here and eat a whole batch of molasses cookies. Those cookies are some good, though. Momma gave me that recipe after I got married. Mine would never turn out as good as hers, though. There was a little something missing. Even Colin could tell the difference. And then one day I was watching her make them, I was holding Dawn, she was just a baby then, and didn't I see her take the teapot and dump some cold tea in the dough.

"Oh, I always put tea in," she said.

"You never told me that," I said.

"That's because it's not in the recipe," she said.

That was Momma for you. She gave me all her recipes like that, in dribs and drabs.

15

Good thing the lamp was on because it'd be as dark as the Number Two in here. Not that I mind the dark. Sometimes I'll sit in my chair after supper and I'll start to reminiscing. About Nana's house in Brook Village, and that little heifer I loved, Sweetie Pie. I remember the smells; the pantry when you came in the back door. And mothballs. Nana used to put them everywhere, even in the yard to keep away snakes. When Jessie was little she popped one into her mouth like a peppermint. Momma was some mad that time. She and Nana never got along.

Then I picture all the rooms in our house, what colour the walls were, the oilcloth. Sometimes I try to remember the names of my teachers, or my favourite dresses. The green brocade I gave to Jessie, the yellow satin I bought for Isaac and Margie's wedding. Colin liked me to have pretty dresses, he was good like that.

And then I come to and I'm sitting in the dark and when I turn on the lamp it's half-past ten and I've forgotten to take my pills.

…blessed art thou among women and blessed is the fruit of thy womb Jesus holy Mary mother of God pray for us sinners now and at the hour of our death amen.

Just my luck my home care was here yesterday morning. She won't be back until next Tuesday now. I can't think who else will come until then except the paperboy – what's his name again, he has this queer name I can never remember – but he'll just go away if I don't answer the door. I was going to make him some fudge today.

Maybe somebody will wonder why the lights are on. Maybe somebody will knock on the door or look in the window. To think how scared I was of that, growing up. As soon as the sun went down I went around the house and closed all the curtains. Once when I'd forgotten the one behind Poppa, Margie snuck outside and put her face in the window and I near had a fit. Poppa made us both go to bed that time.

Life sure is funny. Never thought that one day I'd be praying to see a face in the window. It's like Poppa used to say when I didn't want to eat my potatoes. One day you'll want to eat potatoes real bad and you won't be able to. Or when I didn't want to go to bed at night he'd say: One day you'll want to go to bed but you won't be able to. He was right about that one. Poor Poppa.

…you alone are the Lord you alone are the most high Jesus Christ with the Holy Spirit in the glory of God the father amen.

I had a dream about Willy of all people. We were going somewhere in a car but I was the one doing the driving. I can't remember the last time

I drove a car. I wish you would know when it was the last time you were doing something. The last time you hold a baby in your arms. The last time you dance. The last time you wake up with someone beside you.

My mouth feels like all the juice has been sucked out. The blood seems to have dried over my eye, though. I must look a sight. Funny I'm not hungry. But I'm cold now that I've wet my drawers. Good Lord…That draft under the door doesn't help. I've been after the housing commission to fix it but they won't come unless there's a flood or something. Or the roof caves in. I should have asked Willy. But I don't want to bother him with every little thing. Although he loves it when I ask him, I can tell. I just don't want him thinking I owe him.

Like when I got him to help me move the couch. I had made some fish cakes so I asked him if he wanted to stay for supper. He loves fish cakes, he had four of them! he sure eats a lot for the size of him – my father used to say that was the sign of a strong man – and I had just turned on the radio, the Ceilidh was about to come on, and I was standing at the sink making the tea, thinking how nice it was to have someone to eat with (that's what I mind the most about living by myself) and then didn't he go and ruin it. He was after getting the Carnation out of the fridge and when he went by his hands brushed my arse. I knew it was no accident. I'd seen it coming. Just the way he looked at me sometimes. And a joke he made once about us having a pyjama party. I grabbed the mixing bowl – Colin's aunt Dolly gave it to us when we got married, it weighs a ton, and dropped it into the sink. The dishwater splashed up my front and it broke one of my best teacups, the one with the Cape Breton tartan, but it was worth it, he got the message. I want things to stay just the way they are between us.

A couple of years after Colin died Dawn told me she wouldn't be hurt if I got re-married. I had to laugh. I'd have to be out of my mind to get married again. Some old fart sitting on his arse watching TV all day and hollering for his supper? No thank you! Dawn hasn't figured that out yet. She's not too smart in the man department. At least she doesn't marry them anymore; that was a waste of money.

….lead us not into temptation but deliver us from evil for thine is the kingdom and the power and the glory for ever and ever amen. It's the time of day I used to hate. You've been awake for God knows how many hours, staring into the dark, turning this way and that, thinking maybe if I lie on my stomach I'll fall asleep, that worked once, maybe if I put the pillow here, and everyone in the house snoring, the whole world sleeping, why wouldn't they be? except maybe the nurses at the hospital, and then finally you see it, the bit of grey coming in around the blinds and you know it's over, you've gone and lost one more night, what's wrong with you that you can't sleep, everyone can sleep, and then sometimes I'd feel sorry for myself and start to cry and Colin would wake up and sigh.

Funny about dreams. It was like Poppa was right here beside me. The way he was before the Parkinson's. He was looking for his glasses and then he turned to me and said: "There's something else."

That's the school bus going by. Must be quarter past.

Oh well, at least I'm used to waiting. Had thirty seven years of practice with Colin, more if you count when we were courting. I'd sit on the steps of Momma's house at the Corner and look out for the dust on the road. I don't know how many times I thought he'd stood me up. And after we were married, all those hours waiting in the car. "I'll only be a minute" he'd say, and he'd go in to Levi Leblanc's. The middle of nowhere, I didn't know a body there and there's nothing I hate worse than a hardware store anyway. He was always late for supper. Dawn and I would wait and wait. I knew she was hungry but that's how I was brought up; you didn't eat until Poppa sat down at the table.

One Thanksgiving I had dinner all ready – I always cooked a turkey even after Momma and Poppa died, and it was quarter to six and he was still at the Legion. He loved the Legion; not the liquor as much as the company of men. At home it was just Dawn and me. Even the cat was a girl.

The fixings were all made; the mashed carrots, the turnips, the parsnips – Colin loved parsnips, the cranberry sauce and his mother's mashed potato dressing, I didn't care for it myself, but he and Dawn did – and the longer we waited, the crankier I got.

At quarter past six I went to the pantry and took that yellow platter I always hated and started to carve the turkey. I piled it all on; white meat, dark meat, a leg, stuffing, mashed potatoes, a ton of gravy. Dawn said "What're you doing, Ma?" but I said nothing, just took the platter and walked out the door still wearing my apron. Everyone in town had eaten already and the streets were starting to fill up but I was too mad to care if anyone saw me. I crossed Central Avenue and walked down to the door of the Legion and banged on it with my foot.

Colin got up as soon as I walked in.

"Sit down." I said, and I stood over him with the plate all sticky and the gravy turning to jelly on my hands – I got an awful burn but I didn't feel it until later – and he moved some beer bottles to make room on the table. He was sitting with Jack MacDonnell and Tommy Spoon, and neither one of them opened his mouth, the place was dead calm, and I put the whole thing in front of him and said: "Here's your Thanksgiving Dinner."

The bells are ringing for Jake MacInnis's funeral. Poor Jake. He lived an awful long time after that accident. But he was never right in the head. You'd see him walking upstreet talking to himself; he always seemed to be looking for something. Big handsome man he was too, what a shame.

I haven't been to a funeral in years. Almost everyone I grew up with is dead now, all my sisters gone except Ella and the last time I called her she didn't know who I was. There's not a soul remembers me when I was young. I look at my pictures, how pretty I used to be. Although I didn't think so at the time; I thought my nose was too long and my ankles were fat. I had Poppa's colouring; never had to put rouge on my cheeks. And Momma's wavy hair. Now people look at me and all they see is this ugly old woman looks like a man. Most of them don't even know my name.

The last funeral was Catherine's next doors. I should have gone but it had rained and I was scared I'd fall on the ice. And we were never friends anyway. She didn't like to play cards and she wasn't a talker. I went over a couple times after she moved but she never even offered me a cup of tea. Just sat in her rocking chair all day long. Her son and his wife came last week to empty out the unit. They live in North Sydney but they never used to visit much. Can't say as I blame them.

…you alone are the most high Jesus Christ with the Holy Spirit in the glory of God the Father amen. I can see heat waves coming off that burner. It looks like the pavement in the summer. Or the top of Momma's coal stove. Nothing burns hotter than coal. I get lonesome for it when I smell it outside; there's still a few in town burning it. Good thing I was able to push the kettle off with my cane. God knows I ruined enough kettles in my life. "You'll burn the place down some day" Colin would say. "And you're costing me a fortune." Dawn got me an electric one, the kind that shuts itself off. I only ever use it when she visits. The thing's a darned nuisance; the water's never hot when you want it and it takes up too much space on the counter. You don't get much of a counter in the units. They figure you don't need to cook once you're old.

…holy Mary mother of god pray for us sinners now and at the hour of our death amen let me just have one more cup of tea. The nectar of the gods, that's what Colin always called it. It used to get on my nerves. He was particular about his tea; it had to be King Cole and the milk always had to go in first. Canned milk for Mister Fancy Pants. He hated it when I called him that! I've always been partial to Red Rose myself. It's whatever you've been brought up on.

I dreamed Momma was hollering for me to get up. It was winter and

I was in our little room in the attic, in the bed I shared with Margie and Jane. And Blaise, after Peter got sick and he had to have his own room. You'd see your breath up there when you woke up. Frost on the ceiling. The chamber pot frozen. We'd get up on our tiptoes and take our clothes downstairs and take turns dressing in front of the stove.

I haven't thought about Peter in years. I don't remember him at all before he was sick. They never knew what he had. Momma says it was something with his blood. Cancer, probably. He had these terrible headaches. He'd be so cross with us: "Tell them to be quiet, Momma."

Her oldest son. And nothing she could do.

Maybe Dawn will call. I don't know if she'll twig if I don't answer the phone. She'll think I'm in the bathroom, or I'm not wearing my hearing aid, or lying down or something. Well, I am lying down. Been here so long my arse'll make a dent in the cushion floor.

It's been a while since she phoned me. I've got it marked on the calendar.

She only ever calls when things are going good so I figure she must be having trouble with the new fellow. I just about died when she sent me his picture. She'd been saying Baden this and Baden that and I thought it was a queer name but all along I was imagining an Englishman, I don't know why. But no; as black as the ace of spades.

"Where's he from?" I said the next time she called.

"Calgary," she said.

"But where does he come from?" I said.

"He's from Calgary, ma."

She knew darned well what I meant but she wouldn't answer me.

Willy says it could be worse, she could be living with another woman, like his sister Janet's daughter.

Willy's good about calling. The phone rings every morning at eight thirty sharp.

"How're we doing this morning?" he says.

He has this high voice, whiny like. Must have driven poor Nettie round the bend.

"Oh, sticking together," I say, and he laughs. "And how's hisself?"

"Oh, can't complain, can't complain," and then he always adds: "No one listens anyway."

He'll have been up for hours already, watching the news on TV and listening to the scanner. But he always waits until eight-thirty to call me because he knows how much I like to sleep in.

"You're just a lazybones," he says, but I tell him what Momma always said, that a real lazybones gets up early so he'll have more time to do nothing. That always gets his goat.

After that he gives me all the news: Dougalda MacLean won the jackpot in Mabou and a woman in Philadelphia killed her six children and set her house on fire, or some truck driver in Florida drove into a swamp and survived three days underwater. Then he tells me all the scores; the Leafs lost again – he loves to tell me that, and that they're calling for freezing rain or there's a storm surge or something. If I never turned on the radio I'd still know everything that was going on.

That's all the excuse they'll need to put me in the manor now. Dawn will be glad; she's been after me for five years to move there. Last place I want to go; it smells like piss and all you see are old people in wheelchairs drooling. You look out one window and you see the hospital, you look out the other and you see the cemetery: your future's right there in front of you. Willy's with me on that one. He says the only way he's going there is kicking and screaming.

Poor Willy, I hope he'll get a good report.

Oh holy Saint Jude, apostle and martyr…

THE BABY

Adrian didn't see the doodles right away. Because after he hung up he had stared at the mute black screen of the computer monitor. Then at his hands, palms down on the desk. He had examined them with curiosity and some distaste, as he would have some dead fish on the lake shore. His big hairy slabs of hands, the same ones that went right to work as soon as he got on the phone – brain otherwise occupied, let's party!: In the margins of letters or intake forms, on the covers of file folders, on the scratch pads Anita made for them out of recycled paper. The doodles always surprised him. Some he found beautiful or humorous, others silly, or too revelatory. The funny thing was that he couldn't produce them consciously, had tried a few times but didn't know where to start. He took the best ones home and pinned them on the refrigerator door. Not that Beth appreciated them. He had heard her say to her mother; "Oh, that's just Adrian. I have *no* idea." The rest he destroyed at the end of the day; he didn't want his colleagues finding them, the cleaner thinking; boy oh boy they don't work them too hard in that office, especially that big fellow…

This time the doodles were tame: A procession of monk-like creatures under a bank of inky clouds. A garland of strange leaves. Patricia, underlined twice. Baby, with flourishes and curlicues. He crumpled the page into a tight ball and dropped it in the mesh basket beside his desk.

Outside his office, the hallway was shadowy and hushed. The soles of his shoes squeaked behind him. He counted the squeaks; seventeen, eighteen, nineteen. All the lights were on in the staff room but it was empty too, the floor under the coat rack a jumble of shoes, the table covered with newspapers and flyers and lipstick-stained mugs. The air smelled of spent coffee grounds and microwave popcorn.

In the dark blind window panes his reflection pulled on a parka and boots, set the alarm and walked out.

His was the only vehicle in the parking lot. The pavement stretched out before him a shiny black in places from the salt, mottled beige and white elsewhere. He kicked at one of the brown clumps of slush that fall from the wheel wells of cars in the winter; it was hard and unyielding and his toes throbbed as he sat at the wheel waiting for the windshield to defrost. His shoulders were hunched and tense from the cold.

From where he sat, everything seemed false and treacherous; the slushy streets, the store fronts gaudy with Christmas decorations, people walking fast, bent against the wind. The sad promises of a Friday night.

As he drove, he remembered another winter.

The second-floor apartment on Geneva Street, so cold that they wore tuques to bed, and always full of people: Colleen and Aziz, who lived downstairs, Patricia's friends from the women's shelter, the pink-haired landlady from Malta. He was in graduate school that year, working part-time for Children's Aid.

The decision had been easy: Patricia had been taking birth-control pills for ten years and she smoked; a vasectomy was less of a procedure than a tubal; and if they changed their minds, they could always adopt.

His doctor had been the only one who needed convincing.

Beth closed the front door behind her, dropped her tote bag on the floor and pulled off one of her boots.

"T.G.I.F.!" she said, hobbling to the counter to give Adrian a hug. Her hair felt cold against his cheek. It smelled of car exhaust.

She looked at the mound of potato peelings in front of him, the bottle of wine already half-empty.

"Bad day?" she said.

She was used to it. He had been having a plague of bad days. They spilled over into his evenings, gnawed at his weekends.

"Sort of." He pointed to the pot in the sink. It was full to the brim of naked dirt-streaked potatoes. "Think we'll have enough?"

"What is it?" Beth said.

She sat on one of the stools at the counter.

"I got a call from Pat just before I left the office."

"And?"

"She's pregnant."

"Oh," Beth said.

He turned on the tap and began to rinse the potatoes. They felt cool and slippery in his hands.

"She knew I'd see her at the party tomorrow. She didn't want to surprise me, I guess."

A sliver of potato flesh wedged itself under one of his fingernails. He winced.

"She's getting a bit old to have a baby," Beth said.

Adrian shrugged.

"When is she due?"

"I think she said March."

Beth walked back to the door, pulled off her boot and placed it beside the other one on the mat. She hung her coat in the closet, took her lunch kit out of her tote bag and set it beside the breakfast dishes on the counter.

"What are we eating besides potatoes?" she said.

Later that night as he sat in bed reading, Adrian looked at his wife sleeping beside him; her eyes covered with a mask, her short frosted scruff of hair, her gold earrings, always the same, catching the lamp light.

Beth was also a woman who did not want children. Where did he find them all? Maybe she too would get the urge to have a baby some day. Would she seek out another man then? He had worried about this before, late at night when his imagination unleashed the host of calamities that could befall him. He had always welcomed these specters, irrationally believing that he defused their power by conjuring them up. The thing was not to be caught by surprise.

One Friday night Adrian had woken from a relatively untroubled adolescence to the sight of his mother, whom he had always known as tidy and contained and modest, shaking beside his bed, a wild woman with her black hair loose, great sloppy breasts and white belly quivering under her yellow nylon nightgown: His father, with whom he had argued after supper about nothing, his father was dead.

For years afterwards he would wake up during the night with his heart thumping hard and fear churning in his belly. The house would be warm and silent, the air thick and odorous with the dark mysterious sleep of his family. He knew that downstairs the front and back doors were locked against intruders, the appliances were unplugged and the light on the smoke detector blinked at regular intervals. There was no danger, all was well. But he could not fall back asleep. He had not been watchful once, and he had been blind-sided. He would not let it happen again.

Adrian went to the party alone. Beth disliked the social worker functions; she said that everyone analyzed and psychiatrized. That they drank too much, smoked and talked too much. All true.

It was Pat's turn to host. She lived in a bungalow near the lake with her husband Bill and a million knick-knacks. On Adrian's first visit, Bill had given him the tour of his treasures, expatiating on the merits of the common people's art – a true reflection of North American culture, bla bla bla, and on the thrill of the hunt and capture. He spent his week-ends at garage sales and in second-hand shops. The rest of the time he was a mining engineer.

Two fresh victims were getting the guided visit when Adrian arrived. He nodded at Bill and made his way to an empty armchair at the other end of the room. Everyone was drinking wine and he felt a little self-conscious with his bottle of scotch but that only lasted until the third drink.

He listened to the music – some half-decent jazz, not Bill's pick, he was sure of that, and to the buzz of conversation around him. His ears caught random words: Heat pump. Psycho-dynamic. Control freak. Tuscany.

He looked around for Pat, curious to see what she looked like now that she was pregnant. He had always felt a little repulsed by pregnant women and had never thought about them in a sexual way. But now he found himself wondering what it would be like to make love with one. How did you get around the belly, he wondered, the intruder between?

He didn't see her until she was beside him, perching on the arm of his chair.

"You're getting drunk," she said. "You haven't spoken to two people yet, you're just sitting there getting drunk."

"It's a party," Adrian said.

"You're upset, I knew you would be upset."

"What did I do now?"

"Oh come on. Sitting there like you're at a funeral. How do you think it makes me feel?"

"Guilty?"

"This has nothing to do with you, Adrian. We made that decision as a couple, and now we're not a couple."

"Oh, is that the line? Who came up with that gem? Bill?"

"Fuck. Off," she said.

Watching her walk away, he thought of how little the pregnancy had transformed her. She was tall and sturdy, with large hands and feet that she had always hated. A big belly did not look out of place on her body.

He topped up his drink and followed her to the kitchen. She was pouring cranberry juice into a glass when he came up beside her.

"Don't tell me Bill's got you off the scotch, now," he said.

Jennifer Bridge walked in then, holding an empty wine glass.

"Doesn't she look gorgeous," Adrian said to her, pointing to Pat with his chin.

"Pregnant women always look beautiful," Jennifer said.

"I did not know that," he said.

While Jennifer poured wine into her glass, he leaned close to Patricia, too close, and brushed her ear with his lips.

"I would love to see you with no clothes on," he whispered.

Pat set her glass on the counter hard and walked away. He shrugged at Jennifer, swallowed the rest of the scotch and returned to the armchair. He poured another drink. What the hell, he thought. He'd call a cab, come back for the car the next day.

He was leaving the cream and sage bathroom, having stared at his swaying reflection in the mirror as he washed his hands, having struggled a little with the doorknob on his way out, when he saw Pat entering a room at the end of the hall. He stepped in behind her.

They stood facing each other in a large bedroom with dark brown furniture and pale blue carpeting. The bed was covered with coats and jackets but otherwise the room was neat. Bill, he thought. Pat had always been messy.

"I think you should be going home, Adrian," she said. "I'll call you a cab."

"Come on, let's talk for a minute," he said.

"I don't think it's a good time."

"Patty-Cake," he said, looking into her eyes. She had small bright blue eyes with short thick lashes.

"Patty-Cake," he said again.

She sighed. He saw her features soften, the blue of her eyes become brighter.

They had done this so many times; argued and reconciled in other people's bedrooms, on street corners and park benches and bar stools, and it felt so familiar and so real that for a second it was as if he had dreamed their separation and divorce. Beth, Bill. All the years he had lived without her.

The bedroom door opened and Bill appeared. He looked surprised when he saw Adrian.

"You okay, hun?" he asked Pat.

"Yeah, it's okay," she said.

"All right" he answered, but he did not look convinced. After he left, Pat moved some jackets and sat on the bed. She sighed again: "God I feel like a smoke. I had to quit that too."

Adrian sat beside her and took her hand.

"I know I'm a jerk," he said.

"You do it on purpose; walk in here with a big bottle of scotch. Alone. Where's Beth?"

"She went out with her sister."

"You shouldn't have come without her."

He shrugged.

"I know it can't be easy for you. But what was I supposed to do? Ask for your permission? Your forgiveness? Is that what you want?"

"I already told you what I want," he said quietly.

He saw the dismay in her eyes, the disappointment. He went on anyway; "I'm serious."

Patricia stood up beside the bed. Lifting her hands to her nape she began to undo the buttons on her tunic. She looked away from him as she slid the garment over her head and dropped it on the pile of coats. Her black trousers had a panel of stretchy fabric in the front that went up over her belly button. She pulled it down.

The globe of her abdomen appeared.

It had the hard lustre of a boulder under water, the taut pink surface marbled with the pale blue tributaries of veins. A brown stalk ran down the middle to the stubby flower of her navel, and a red wave intersected it where the waistband of her pants had been. Her breasts looked heavy.

She caught his look; "The bra too?" She looked amused.

Adrian shook his head. He picked up the tunic and held it out for her. She lifted her arms, turned around so he could push the gold buttons through the buttonholes. It reminded him of the summer that she had dislocated her shoulder and needed help to get dressed.

They sat side by side on the bed.

"Are you happy now?" she asked him.

"Are you happy?" he answered.

"Yes. I am."

"That's good," he said. "I'm glad."

After a while, she said: "I'll call you a cab."

"No," he said, getting up. "It's not a bad night. I'll walk."

He closed the door of the bedroom and crossed the hallway with exaggerated care, not wanting to appear drunk. Across the room Bill gave him a quizzical look. His bearded face looked young, the set of his mouth uncertain. Adrian winked at him as he shrugged on his coat.

He adjusted the collar, felt his pockets for his gloves, and stepped out into the winter night.

La Quarantaine, Elaine Amyot, 1990

Beth McLaughlin

HEALTHY COMMUNITIES – GREEN, ECO, SUSTAINABLE, SMART ETC – COMING ON THE SCENE!

Dear Reader,

How many of you are getting impatient with the hit and miss efforts of our municipalities to deal with climate change? Why aren't they focusing all their actions toward improving the quality of life, clean air and clean water, for their citizens – is that your thinking? Why aren't those who represent us considering their own children, and what should be done? How many of you have discussed climate change with your heirs and their future? A few North American towns and cities are doing things differently in an overall way – limiting sprawl, taking into consideration the extent of their water supply, building in structures for citizen consultation, changing our attitudes toward public transport. How many are working toward the simple goals of clean air and water which will align their decisions and policies from issues of economic development to greening their communities? Local levels of government seem simply to be expecting that individuals will do their part with little leadership from the municipality – and important level of government because their areas of responsibility affect us most directly. When are we going to realize that climate change is real?

This series of articles will outline each of the five pillars of a healthy community, with examples of action taken by entire communities in Canada. Most have been due to the push of a small group or a municipal leader, to respond to environmental, social and economic concerns. Because "sustainable" is such an overused word, let's call ours the 'healthy community' instead.

The Healthy Community Movement, a.k.a. the "Green," "Sustainable," "Cool," or "Ecological" Communities, and "Smart Growth" movement, has been brewing for many decades. However, we should note that our "throwaway"society has never been more "productive" in tossing "stuff" – until a short 40 years ago, everything was reused, recycled. Food was sold in bulk, wrapping of many products was unheard of. Remember "built-in obsolescence"? Our values changed – and are changing again.

The rise of this ecological movement has its distant origins in the middle to late 1800's. During that time, the growth of cities and the swallowing up of farmlands in the US and Canada prompted people to call for "green islands." These consisted of restful places for people in cities and preserved access to peaceful places in the countryside. Those parks didn't just happen: people demanded and pushed for their creation because of their concern for what was happening around them.

By the 1890s, a British court journalist, Ebenezer Howard, provoked by the horrible living conditions in parts of London, designed and proposed the "Garden City." It consisted of a series of small towns surrounded by an agricultural belt, to provide food for the residents. Two cities in England were founded: Letchworth Garden City in 1903 and Welwyn Garden City in 1920. They thrive today.

More recently, the problems encountered by cities have encouraged the existence of the Healthy Community Movements. These include the car with its need of four parking spaces (home, work, groceries and recreation), its emissions and sprawl, along with the infrastructure demands and costs of new streets, roads, water and sewer, electricity, waste management, and inadequate public transport. Despite different perspectives and motivations, these movements promote similar solutions – always toward clean air and therefore, clean water.

Remember the Bruntland Commission? It was set up to respond to the emerging concern for the environment in European cities in the 1980s. The "Green Cities" movement was a result of this interest. The "Ecological City" proposes new ways of maintaining and restoring the balance between the natural and the built environment in urban settings. Smart Growth's principle drive is good planning: the ability to find the best use of land while ensuring quality of life. The "Healthy Cities" movement was begun by the World Health Organization in 1985. It spread like a brushfire through Europe, Australia and the US.

In Canada, the City of Vancouver commissioned Mark Roseland (in the late eighties!) to find ways to deal with climate change. The Clouds of Change report was submitted in 1990. In 1992, Winnipeg urban planner Marcia Nozick published "No Place Like Home." In Ontario, Dr. Trevor Hancock began writing and speaking tours in communities concerned with taking some control over what their towns and cities would look like in the future.

Since then, Vancouver, Hamilton, Moncton and other Canadian communities have set their sights on becoming healthier communities.

What are the earmarks of the healthy community? Great social vitality, land conservation efforts, a strong urban-rural relationship, the reduction of pollution and energy conservation characterize one. Economic development, the creation of local wealth, and the development of cultural potential are essential. Access by all to our pooled resources such as rinks, parks, community centres, clubs, and aquatic centres, churches, city halls, libraries and schools, colleges and universities are equally basic to the healthy community.

The five pillars of a healthy collectivity are Design, Planning and Transportation, Community Culture, Living within the Limits of the Environment, Creating Local Wealth and more Participative Governance.

Design, Planning and Transportation

Our children are worried that our air is getting dirtier and that we adults are doing nothing about it. They have little faith that we can change our behaviour to deal with climate change, says research from the U de Moncton. Are we unable to act or react because the entire subject is overwhelming and we don't know where to start? Entire cities have pulled together to stop sprawl, limit water consumption, clean up their air, improve energy efficiency, set up groups for short and long-term projects and a whole bunch of other things and you in the suburbs can be saved! You will read about them in this series. But first, let's agree on one goal for a future Healthy Community: that our children and grandchildren will be able to breathe cleaner air in 20 years, rather than the contrary by continuing along our same track.

Can you make the connection between your grandchildren gasping for air and business as usual in our cities for the last 50 years? Children using puffers are at 20-25% now. Want to do things differently? First, can you picture the main street of your original downtown: buildings close together or attached, living quarters above stores and other types of homes nearby. Schools, stores and services centralized, allowing people to walk and requiring little need for a vehicle. This is a community layout deliberately organized to consume fewer resources and produce less pollution of the natural environment. The plan includes community centers, parks and shared areas for recreation. Gardening and socializing are also thoughtfully part of it. We can't go back, some people say! Is this back we ask? Are we so spoiled or so limited in our own possibilities as to choose the same fouled nest? Twenty years from now, healthy modes of transportation for pedestrians, cyclists and wheelchairs, simultaneously contributing to air quality, will help slow down the speeded-up life we are now living. In big cities, several compact, whole communities already make up the larger picture (think of neighbourhoods of Montreal and Toronto). For a really healthy future, a good relationship between urban and the nearby rural communities, the latter providing fresh meat, fish, cheeses and vegetables for all, while the new urban businesses supply us with all the equipment required for these enterprises and more, are part of the picture. Moncton has a couple of spaces for community gardening, meeting others and having fun. Urban market food production is a phenomenon just waiting to happen!

Making the most of the sun, the wind and the rain means using passive solar energy (provided your building is oriented to capture the sun, and has natural radiators (windows) to capture energy. What's better than free heat in winter? In summer, close the blinds! The breezes cool your building in summer and in winter, those forces are minimized by a few well-placed deciduous trees and the buildings nearby. Why recover rainwater? Because it nourishes your garden, the flowers and our lawns. Free again! Why use your metered drinking water for your garden? The land also filters rain water while recharging groundwater (our wells). Natural or manmade ditches (swales), seen throughout Dieppe, absorb the rain and slow the runoff to our rivers too.

Beauty, in design and in architecture, is also part of the "healthy community." Ever been to Paris, London or Sydney Australia? Beauty is not accidental or restrained to an individual building there. In his book, "Places of the Soul," Christopher Day explains how architecture reflects the history, age, ethnic origins and values of the community. He talks about the uniqueness and authenticity of our cities as shown in our "built environment." After all, how interesting is a city which looks like every other city built with the same materials, same stores? Our eye notes streetscapes – what an attractive street that is – as well as individual buildings. The City of Fredericton, for example, put in place a policy to have new construction in the downtown harmonize with the existing architecture of the late 1800s. They also have recently come to the rescue, with partners, to preserve a lovely older building in their city centre. So why don't more municipal governments act to preserve their authenticity?

Architecture affects our health. We know about sick buildings – off-gassing, poor ventilation, mold. Christopher Day (Places of the Soul, 1990) writes that material used in design and construction should contribute to our health and well-being while minimizing pollution. Building codes can include beauty, why not materials and the natural elements?

City or Town Design, Including Transportation

But, you say, we can't just redesign the whole city! Ever seen such an attractively designed area that you just had to get out and walk around? So how do we get there? Remember our goal of cleaner air in 20 years. We begin by working to reduce the number and distance of vehicle trips between where we live and where we work, study, shop for food, play and pray. Streetscapes, an interesting combination of old and new, houses closer together, services available within walking distance, reducing parking at malls while improving bus service, parks – these are what make you get out of your car! That's how we reduce our burning of fossil fuels and improve air quality. By taking an inventory of services in each neighbourhood, and a policy of better integrated planning – mixed use planning, within limits – we identify what is missing in the area. We then insert, for example, a grocery store or a school.

Many cities are finding ways of reducing the need for vehicles. How? Vancouver has a policy of no more new roads. They have chosen instead to build alternative modes of transportation, such as the Sky Train and bicycle lanes. Calgary requires developers to do "infilling" in the downtown area. Montreal is in the process of getting 4,000 vehicles annually off their roads for a ten-year period, by providing alternate means of transportation and improved public transport. Charlottetown, in 2007, won an award for instituting a public transportation system, city-wide, which, in a costing exercise, they found to be less expensive than building and operating a downtown parking garage! The five bus fleet consists of "vintage style" trolleys, in keeping with the historic character of the city. Ridership surpassed expectations by 40%. Each bus can replace 40 cars.

Lots of cities, including Moncton and Dieppe, are working on the construction of alternate transportation, walking and wheeling routes linked to services. Although this project seems to be stalled in Moncton, to be effective, these routes are connected to shopping, recreation areas and schools. Since walkers and bikers often choose these alternate methods for their health, they don't want to be breathing the bus dust! In Metro Moncton, there is much which can be done including changing our attitudes: More bus transportation to high density work areas like hospitals, universities, the downtown, call centres, will contribute to lowering the number of vehicles on the road. Some cities go as far as giving FREE bus passes to employees (but obtaining their commitment first). Universities are starting to include a bus pass with the student fees, as this practice helps to lower the institution's real costs for parking, maintenance and snow removal (we in Moncton know a bit about that!). High-occupancy vehicles (HOVs), carpoolers, are given parking priority and lower rates in some communities. In such a project, participants often start with a commitment to carpool only once or twice a week. All these actions bring about the overall reduction of energy use and greening the city, with a result of better air quality.

Finally, the Canadian Institute of Planners (the professional association of urban, environmental and rural planners) now proposes a three step planning process:

1)Envisioning by citizens of their ideal community
2)Development of general objectives by these same people
3)Enunciation of basic principles to steer that process

June 2006, the City of Moncton organized a two-day visioning exercise. One hundred participants looked at the downtown area and what they want to see there…a fine beginning. But our community discussions on the future of the entire surface area of our region will ideally last a lifetime. Changes will happen with or without our input. So why not get involved and have a say? The planning is not finished when the area is built upon. No…there are still many changes to follow due to reconstruction, demolition, fire, selling vacant land.

Energy and Energy Efficiency

With the present world situation of fossil fuels, as well as the organizational changes that have occurred at NB Power, some municipalities are moving toward becoming their own energy providers. Edmundston, for example, acquired a small hydroelectric power plant, to be upgraded and integrated into their power needs. Others have historically maintained a local power company (Saint John, Perth-Andover). An Irving company recently purchased the hydroelectric dam in St. George, NB, and invested to increase its generating capacity. Now, interested municipalities, particularly around the Acadian peninsula, are getting educated about community-based wind energy. Still others are converting assets to the energy efficient method of "district heating." In such a system, a big institution, such as a municipal building, hospital or university, recovers its waste heat (steam, for instance) and shares it with surrounding buildings, such as residences or commercial buildings. Charlottetown, PEI, has had a district heating system for 30 years. Halifax has committed to a district energy project. Word has it that a district heating project is in the works in Moncton. Cogeneration, where surplus heat or steam is captured and converted to electricity, is being used in at least one giant wood-processing mill in St. Leonard, NB. Industrial and commercial energy audits, followed by overhauling of older machines and retrofitting buildings, can ratchet up savings, reduce CO_2 emissions and make for cleaner air, our main goal.

Energy efficiency is also built-in simply by angling the solar and wind orientation of new buildings a few degrees. Combined with proper use of windows and doors as radiators in winter (and shade in summer), passive solar can save up to one third of our heating requirements. Studies on solar heating conducted in residential multi-storey dwellings in Halifax suggest that buildings between four to seven stories high have the potential of meeting all of their space and water heating requirements from solar energy.(see Further reading) "The Right-to-Light" and zoning by-laws which address building orientation support this. Barcelona mandated that solar thermal energy (for hot water) be implemented whenever possible, especially on new construction projects. Steps taken in Barcelona were so successful that they were duplicated in cities throughout Spain. The ordinance was pushed by a group of people committed to Renewable Energies. Why can't that happen here?

Our new Efficiency NB program has residential, commercial and industrial programs to help retrofit buildings to get a bigger bang for our buck by paying less for heating and lighting, cleaner air being a by-product.

Really exciting is the opportunity to get help with an Energy Efficiency Community Campaign! The town of Perth-Andover has embarked on a two-year plan, giving away CFLs (compact fluorescent lights), going door-to-door to educate people on hot water heater blankets (a one-year payback), energy audits of residential, commercial and business buildings. The town of Perth-Andover is leading the way by having seven of their municipal buildings assessed and retrofitted. The energy savings will help finance a FREE swim and skate initiative. Belledune is undertaking an energy efficiency and conservation program. The City of Bathurst, partnering with Bathurst Sustainable Development (a group of committed citizens whose projects over the past 8 years have been legion) has recently announced an Energy Efficiency Campaign with Efficiency NB. 24 municipalities, groups and churches are in the process or have completed projects with the help of Efficiency NB. These projects include retrofitting and lighting improvements of commercial and municipal buildings. Buildings such as hotels, restaurants, office buildings, churches, grocery stores, schools, hospitals and university buildings, large multi-unit residences, recreational facilities (arenas, for example) qualify for advice and financial aid.

Just recently a new program to help medium and small manufacturers was launched. There are programs and financial help for new commercial buildings to build greener too. Though NB has very good building codes, we can always improve. A few builders have begun to set their standards to the Energuide bar – see Success Stories on Efficiency NB's website.

The City of Moncton, in the last decade, did undertake a retrofit program for some of our assets, notably the arenas. And we have a fleet of Smart Cars rather than gas-guzzling vans. But remember, our tax dollars in all municipalities help pay for the heat and lights – as well as the vehicles owned by them. As electricity costs rise, where is the leadership by our local governments to reduce our costs and help clean our air?

Water Supply

Remember the hydrologic cycle of evaporation and condensation (which we all studied in Grade 5)? Ever heard the story of raining frogs? Of course, you have seen the black flecks of pollution sitting on the snow! Need more be said about the relationship of water and air? Protecting the drinking water supply, quantity and quality, is part of every city's plan. But in a survey by Environment Canada in 2001, 24.5% of the responding municipalities indicated that they experienced water shortages. This survey also indicated that 25% of responding municipalities reported problems with water quality (boil order!) as well. You can bet that these percentages have not gone down in 7 years so what will it be in 20 years – going the same old route, adding more chemicals to "clean" our water supplies or protecting our water at its source? We used to think ourselves superior to the Europeans who no longer drank water from their taps – they had to buy bottled water. Many European countries began to protect their water at the source – keeping trees standing, stopping runoff from agricultural and industrial operations. Now they drink from the tap again. Some Canadian cities and provinces are starting up Drinking Water Source protection programs.

Remember that underused word: conservation? Ironically, water conservation helps preserve water quality too. How? Waste water –which ends up as grey (shower, sink), black (industrial) and treated water – eventually flows back into "clean water." Some of the content of that water also goes into the air…and comes back down. Recent predictions warn of more water shortages in the future. Climate change brings alternately drought or increased frequency of storms. With the latter therefore, we get increased runoff (industrial, agricultural and municipal streets) into clean water.

Situations, ideas and solutions

Rising sea levels are not coming, they are here – anyone who spends time on the seacoasts of northeastern NB can tell you! Saltwater incursion into the drinking water of at least one coastal community has already occurred in NB.

Water diversion, which involves changing the natural flow of water to another location by using dams, canals, or pipelines, is often suggested to respond to increasing demand. Yet diversion creates drastic problems to the ecosystem from which it is drained. Check out the Colorado River, US and the Aral Sea, Russia.

In recent years, water shortages have usually been due to over-consumption and/or wastage by leaks in old infrastructure (Quebec City saved 25% more water once leaks were identified and repaired!). Charlesbourg, Québec, pop. 72,000 adopted an integrated management approach to their drinking water supply in the 1990s. With more demand on their pristine water supply, and finding water treatment insufficient and costly, they created a team to address water leakages and promote water conservation, largely through water-saving devices in the toilets. Charlesbourg today has one of the lowest costs and highest quality drinking water in Québec. London, ON distributed free water-saving kits to residents more than a decade ago. Moncton sells $15 water-saving kits, an excellent value, at City Hall.

Some municipalities have undertaken community-based management of the drinking water supply by forming a team, identifying sources and potential sources of pollution, creating partnerships to deal with farming (by building earthen walls or berms to keep runoff out, for example) and forestry practices (by making financial arrangements to keep wood standing – Ontario has adopted this practice). This type of management helps spreads the word about good and best practices and through the use of volunteers, involves personal buy-in and responsibility toward the water supply. As with electricity, the more you use, the more you pay – at least, in most jurisdictions. An increasing block-rate structure of cost for water use will help conserve water.

But we are seeing changes: Moncton's City Hall was built with low-flow toilets. Going much farther, the City of Vancouver has implemented new low-volume plumbing codes for all new construction. We are also beginning to see entire towns, such as Battleford, Sask, propose toilet-replacement incentive projects which include a rebate program, rather than investing in new or expanded reservoirs. Fredericton recently offered, in a weekend long pilot project, a $50 rebate for the purchase of a low-flow toilet. In the U.S., exchange programs for old toilets, which are crushed and re-used as paving material, have been set up in many communities concerned with water issues. Water and tax money are saved.

Living in Harmony with the Environment

Our childhood relationship with a corner of the wild (… a vacant lot in an urban setting, the old camp beside the river where your family spent Sundays, a tiny piece of the seashore) is what prompts us to stand up for our environment later on. Children are losing touch with nature, as the book *Last Child in the Woods: Saving our Children from Nature Deficit Disorder* (2005) describes. Just how do we treat our habitat when we have no bond with it or worse, fear it…? Need we be reminded that our ties to the Earth include food and ultimately, cars, paper, clothes, plastics, water and air? Did you know that deforestation is also one of the main causes of climate change? A cornerstone of the healthy community includes greening the community and living within the limits of the environment.

The healing properties of Nature include its ability to deal with pollutants. Moncton's vision exercise of two years ago recommended 'more trees, more trees. But we also know that we've exceeded nature's cleansing capacity by the level of nitrates in our rivers, cosmetic pesticides in our bays, car fumes, boil orders, acid rain, and by the hole in the ozone layer. Throw in "cumulative effects" of these pollutants (the use of chemicals became widespread since World War II – 60 years and counting) it becomes obvious that our accepted practices cannot remain the same.

Restoring natural processes to live in harmony with the environment:

Ian McHarg, landscape architect and urban planner, founder of the Department of Landscape Architecture at the University of Pennsylvania, outlined eight natural processes and their roles in nature in his landmark book, *Design with Nature* (1969). Most apply to Metro Moncton: the role of surface waters, marshes, aquifers, quality agricultural lands, forests and woodlands and steep hills. Sorry – no room to explain here! McHarg stated that the city should be considered an ecosystem, and problems should be approached using this basic idea.

McHarg viewed the city through urban planning eyes, fortified with the roles of nature. His insights included dealing with smog, that phenomenon of low-lying pollutants, using "air corridors" small forests planted where strong breezes or winds predominate. A second benefit of 'air corridors' is the humidity and modifying temperatures provided by those urban forests. McHarg's third recommendation was to use full cost accounting methods, from extraction to landfill, to compare the long term value of what we could lose (ex. agricultural lands) to what we could gain (ex. housing). He also noted these costs usually fall on the public sector while the profits go to the private domain.

Greening and energy use:

Reducing the "heat island effect" of the city by greening lowers air conditioning needs, conserving summer energy use, while absorbing CO_2, and improving water drainage. Nature's services include pollution absorption, flood and erosion control and protection against damaging ultraviolet light.

In an inventory of Canadian energy assets, Torrie Smith and Associates (Ottawa) concluded that simply through energy efficiency and conservation, a 50% reduction of energy use is possible over 25 years (by 2030), thereby also rendering companies more competitive!

For cleaner air, a city plan whose objective is to reduce energy use includes improved construction standards for energy efficiency, less car dependency and better public transport. Investment in local renewable energies (district heating, geothermal, mini-hydro: the latter two developed and manufactured in NB). These, along with wind and solar will yield long term returns of cleaner air: long-term solutions, where the fuel is free and there are no or few waste by-products.

Greening strategies: Water

"...We're actually losing water from the hydrological cycle because rain has to catch something green that can sweat it back into the cycle. It's called transpiration, and we're losing so much plant life to clear-cutting, drought and deforestation, the water (molecule) is simply breaking apart and blowing away." (Maude Barlow, 2008).

Strategies to restore city ecology include planting fruit trees, flowers and herbs. Implement a policy of using indigenous plants requiring little care, rather than exotic species. Simple projects like installing a rain barrel reduce pressures on drinking water reserves (and our pocketbooks) for watering gardens. Sustainable Bathurst organized a rain barrel project several years ago. The Conservation Coop in Ottawa collects grey waters (sink, shower and bath) to reuse for garden irrigation. Green roofs absorb water, reduce the cost of drainage systems and air conditioners, save heating.

Urban brooks, ponds and marshes are often neglected, filled in or covered over (piped). Sound familiar? Their protection and restoration revitalize neighbourhoods. Our linear path along the Petitcodiac is a shining example! Public discussion promotes stewardship and creates new procedures and goals and how to implement them.

Land policies:

What else can we do? Community Gardens are great places to make new friends, trade surplus food. Moncton has had two such gardens, one on the U de Moncton campus, the other near Rocky Stone Field. Post-Carbon Moncton, a local group, is working on urban food production amongst other projects.

The Nature Trust of NB, the NB Community Land Trust and the Nature Conservancy of Canada are groups to which owners can deed over some (or all) of their land to be looked after in perpetuity. The land is preserved for a park, a garden or farm.

Creating Local Wealth

"A community enriches itself by its own existence," said Jane Jacobs, author of *Cities and the Wealth of Nations* (1984) and her recent jewel, *The Nature of Economies* (2000). Creativity, innovation, and flexibility are major keys to successful economic development, observed Jacobs, R. Florida and others. In keeping with our goal of cleaner air for our children and grandchildren, how does business relate to action to deal with climate change? Will municipalities initiate collective action to help local business? Read on.

Jacobs, in line with the ideas of Schumacher, outlines principles for self-sufficiency: 1) Make more with less, maximizing use of existing resources: incorporating conservation, prevention of pollution and recycling. 2) Encourage the circulation of money within our own community, with a goal of 6-8 times.

Don't all these ideas fly in the face of globalization? Why...yes, but we should have a say, *n'est-ce pas*, in the future of our own region? Here are a few things we can all do to help keep our children working at home or starting businesses here.

Doing more with less:

Are our governments and Crown Corporations spending tax money like bigshots or are they working to keep costs down? Has NB Power gone through its own exercise of implementing reduction of energy use, as the Dept. of Environment has? And our other provincial government departments?

NS, BC, PEI and Québec have established a political goal for waste diversion. These policies obliged all government departments and agencies to look for creative ways to meet this goal. Accounting for the full-cycle costs of landfill management of materials, be it dangerous waste or cardboard... it doesn't make sense not to extract and reuse. In 1995, the NS government also tied economic development to waste diversion – which triggered a new way of looking at projects. This vision helped create 1500 new, skilled jobs, many in the manufacturing sector there. NS now diverts 60% of its wastes.

The citizens of Metro Moncton are justifiably proud of the fact that we separate our garbage into wet and dry, composting and extracting many things for recycling. However, we do not yet oblige multiunit dwellings, nor commerce and industry to do the same. At the provincial level, we have not established policies requiring waste diversion, nor is there much separation in the north of the province.

Despite lack of public policy, members of Green Committees of Assomption Vie, the Delta Beauséjour, Spielo –and Forest Glen School (and undoubtedly many other work places) – have taken their own initiative to separate wet and dry, composting and many other actions!

Remanufacturing Saves Energy, Creates Jobs:

The recycling industry rings in five times more jobs and revenue than the simple burial of waste, studies tell us. When economic development is added, the use of those recyclables as "primary stock" in a new product increases the number of skilled and well-paying jobs. We encourage local enterprise by offering "primary stock or supply" – the extracted material – for their business. A cost becomes a revenue, we create jobs, increase our tax base, and add value to our available resources. It costs far less in the life cycle of an element to reuse it than to start from scratch, extracting it from the Earth.

Technologies:

Investing in simple technologies reduces electricity use and fossil fuel consumption. A gadget exists which can control water heaters and reduce energy use from NB Power to our homes. Plugs can stop the phantom draw of electricity – up to 25% of our electricity use – which we have all heard about on the national news recently. Why aren't we implementing these here in NB? HydroQuébec installs devices in Montreal homes warning them of peak electricity consumption times and therefore higher rates. Osage, Iowa invested in these technologies and saved an average of $1000 per home per year in its city!

More measures to improve air quality by reducing electricity use include improving even good building codes and low-volume plumbing codes. Long term and inexpensive measures include planning and policies addressing orientation of buildings to maximize passive solar energy and planting of trees and other greenery for windbreaks in winter and shade in summer.

Keeping money in the community and the province

Newfoundland and Labrador just passed legislation to take back the timber and water rights granted to Abitibi-Bowater in Grand Falls-Windsor, as the latter recently announced a March 2009 closing. This is not the first time the government of NL has taken back their resources or insisted that job creation be linked to projects and some profits be remitted to their province when big business wanted to extract their resources (ie. remember nickel mining in Labrador, oil rights later?). Yet NB allows cutting on our publicly-owned Crown Lands for a year AFTER a mill has closed by those same mill owners and exporting raw logs.

We create local wealth by encouraging money to circulate in our own community and province. Auctioning off NB's natural resources to multinational companies, allowing our natural resources (wind for example) to be developed, not by us, but by more trans-nationals is poor business. We need policies to bolster our economy by doing it ourselves!

Remember: "A community enriches itself by its own existence," declared Jane Jacobs. Here are the remaining principles for self-sufficiency:

3) Substitute imported goods by locally-made goods.
4) Use the already established cultural and economic activities of the area as a springboard for further economic development.
5) Make something new with the resources of the area.

Available local resources:

Halifax mixes roof shingles with asphalt to fill potholes! Mixed paper and newspapers are used in the manufacture of toilet paper elsewhere, so why allow baby maple trees to be used for this purpose in NB? In other regions, innovative thought created green businesses making building insulation, green mulch, cardboard, cat litter and fibreboard using mixed paper, magazines, telephone directories and old newspapers. Elsewhere, broken glass from windshields is integrated into ceramic tiles. Styrofoam beads and egg cartons (polystyrene), plastic containers, (yogurt and sour cream) are reused for new products like hoses and garbage bags. In NB, we re-manufacture plastic bags and pop bottles become little mats. Palettes, utility cables and scrap wood also have real potential for reuse: they can be chipped for fuel or remanufactured.

The remains of Construction and Demolition in some cities never reach the landfill. In Moncton, Habitat for Humanity resells discarded construction materials, from sinks to windows and doors. Furniture is extracted and repaired for resale in certain communities. Calgary and Moncton are experimenting with methane extraction from their old 'dumps'. We do have a provincial car tire deposit for a remanufacture centre in Minto, why not more?

Toyota and Mercedes developed modular, reusable packaging for car parts resulting in million dollar savings.

Our pulp and paper industry is in distress, but there's no obligation by government to reuse some of our paper. Instead, our paper goes to brokers in Ontario who resell it. Yet, Europe and many US states require a certain percentage of recycled content before they purchase paper. Where is our flexibility and innovation?

Still interested in keeping your offspring working in the province?

Another aspect of keeping money in the community is the principle of 'the price is not equal to the cost' – which, interpreted, means that we need to look at the larger picture when making purchases. Marcia Nozick's example described the purchase of a fleet of buses by the City of Winnipeg. Buses were manufactured in Winnipeg and in Québec. Winnipeg decided to buy the Québec–built buses, because they cost 5% less. However, by not taking into account the multiplier effect, in other words, the economic spinoff of the locally-based businesses supplying parts, those dollars left Winnipeg. Creating trust funds for investment in local entreprise also helps keep jobs here.

Substitution of imported goods:

Why not keep and use an inventory of area suppliers for the region's commerce in all areas (thereby reducing energy consumption due to long distance transportation costs) based on the principle that a community enriches itself by its own existence?

Did you know that food we eat daily has travelled an average of a thousand to two thousand kilometers? Keeping in mind Nozick's principle of "the price does not equal the cost," the increasing number of market gardeners and organic farmers in the Metro Moncton area can only help the quality and quantity of good food available. It also contributes to our community's staying economically healthy by creating meaningful employment, assuring a safe food supply (when you can look your supplier in the eye and s/he takes responsibility for their products), improving the urban-rural relationship and being self-reliant. Gardening and gardening supplies are growth businesses!

Other cities, provinces, states and countries are taking charge in these areas. Nova Scotia, BC and very recently NB, have policies to encourage the establishment of businesses for the extraction of dangerous waste, paint, for example, rather than it ending up buried in the dump. In Maine, 15 years ago, the beer industry was made to reuse their bottles, thus creating 1200 jobs. Germany's legislation obliges industries to reduce or take back their own packaging. A levy, imposed either at the beginning or at the end of the manufacturing cycle, is used to create businesses using recycled materials.

In NB, we have yet to develop legislation for local economic benefits with regard to wind energy nor do we have policies to support and promote value-added wood products (flooring, trim, stairs, wood windows and doors, musical instruments, etc.) which create far more skilled employment using our trees than clearcutting forests for making 'virgin paper' and toilet paper.

Cultural businesses:

Last but far from least, as the City of Moncton's Mr. Champoux's first economic development study suggested, investing in the local culture can reap returns. Ecotourism in the historical, cultural and environmental domains is a rapidly growing sector. "Cultural economic activity is the Atlantic provinces is a four billion dollar business, yet we hardly invest in this area," says Arts NB director Pauline Bourque. The entire Green Economy is a growing area for investment and development. The new ECO museum of the Miramichi River is one example. A second is the open history museum of Memramcook.

What the Heck Is 'Community Culture'?

Belonging to a service club, church group, gardening or card-playing club, antique car club, naturalist or environmental group, book clubs, sports leagues: all contribute to the social and economic vitality of the town. A fifth essential aspect of a healthy community is that complex mix of community culture and social ties – which enhance safety and security for all. Moncton, Dieppe and Riverview enjoy very good relationships while belonging to different language groups and sometimes holding different values. A deeper understanding of our own cultures, especially those of the English language (English, German, Irish, Scot) could lead to a greater appreciation of our immediate area. The Mi'maq and Maliseet peoples are strengthening their cultures with the taking back of traditional values and teachings. The resurgence in the pride of Acadian society has resulted in stronger social ties by organizing Les Retrouvailles – giant family reunions. Tracing the origins of their family names, inviting relatives from around the world to come to NB (Acadie) to see their roots and meet their cousins have further consolidated those ties. The World Acadian Congress met here in August, 2009. Meanwhile, Acadians met many times in 2007 to do a thorough inventory of the state of their arts and culture in NB. The recommendations of the Summit on Arts and Culture or Les États Généraux are presently being pursued.

Our culture and heritage are the basis of our authenticity and the true richness of life. It's our uniqueness which makes our community attractive to others and to ourselves. Community culture is, in part, the recognition of those distinguishing elements of our culture(s), what is typical of us: our habits, food, dress, architecture and language. This includes knowing our stories, traditions and arts. It encompasses our favourite natural attractions and knowing the natural history of the area. Think of the other side, where every town has the same stores and looks like every other town – where's the appeal in that?

Getting people involved in envisioning their future necessarily implies meeting new people with some of the same interests you have. Some people will be interested in promoting the unique story of the origins of their town, even neighbourhoods. Others will want to highlight business lineages, survival stories and heritage buildings. What are the aspects we find so appealing in New England and European towns and cities?

Belonging:

Community culture also means making sure that all our citizens feel they belong. Meeting their basic needs: enough to eat, a decent living space, being autonomous are essential. Integrating low-income citizens by having designated units in multi-quartered dwellings or offering a supplement to homeowners for an apartment in their building are two ways of accomplishing this. In Montreal, certain companies organize groups of people, including special needs people, to plan, acquire, renovate to their needs and building codes, all the while enabling them to acquire skills to manage their own cooperative housing buildings. Habitat for Humanity builds houses with the help of their future owners whose own sweat-equity contributes to the capital financing of the home.

Eyes on the street:

Our local constabulary and Jane Jacobs tell us that "eyes on the street" are a contributor to safe neighbourhoods! Mixing of residences, restaurants, shops, and social clubs make safer areas where it's in everyone's interest, merchants and residents alike, to keep the area interesting and friendly. Neighbourhoods where people of all ages with different schedules live in a variety of housing types, single and family units, apartment buildings, all with different schedules, have more 'eyes on the street'. Residents' participation in planning and community management encourages more "eyes on the street." Local involvement also furthers a sense of belonging.

What other methods and actions have cities and towns taken to improve social ties?

University-neighbourhood – city partnerships work on improving tensions which sometimes develop. Time is spent on building interpersonal relationships before the main issues can be addressed. For example, Saint John and the Saint John Museum are researching stories about the "hidden visible social group" the Black people who accompanied the Loyalists back in the 1780s. Think of contrasting neighbourhoods where relations get strained. Below are a few projects which have accomplished much.

Small steps like students getting an oral history of a person, a building or a street from long-time residents, builds bridges between generations. Making videos of the history of a longstanding building improves skills and creates new social connections. Work-study projects where students are put in a new environment make for new attitudes. Mini-courses in landscape architecture, planning and development of physical and esthetic infrastructure, with a follow-up to apply this knowledge to their own neighbourhood, have been successfully used to involve people in their own environs. Churches have set up employment registers and created work through needs of their parishioners. Assessments of economic and social needs, by interviewing people in isolated residential areas, to match skills and employment opportunities can benefit everyone. Parks and recreation areas are often established through citizens' efforts, creating new bonds and cared-for land.

A Healthier Community: More Public Input

Our municipal governments play a big role in planning and urban design, housing standards, public works, the maintenance and creation of parks, and, directly and indirectly, public health. Many issues affect us subtly (cosmetic pesticide use, air quality from industry and pollution from vehicles, lack of access to services due to poor public transport) yet we take less interest, most of the time, in the actions of municipal government than other levels. Placing human development and ecosystem health at the centre of our decision-making will lead us to new ways of thinking and governing our towns and cities, says Ontario Dr. Trevor Hancock. We will take more control over our urban living conditions. But, these new ideas imply changes in the role of local government. We'll need new policies regarding the physical and social environment, all the while involving the public in the decision-making process.

Often, groups get together to protest or stop a project. Why not be consulted prior to a development getting underway (from aquatic centres to housing complexes to new businesses) for ideas and suggestions which could make the project acceptable – or not? The success of the creation of the healthy city requires the participation, the vision and the will of its citizens, declared Lewis Mumford, urban planner and author of the *City in History* (1938) among two dozen books. Change, with the participation of the public, is more likely to succeed. A two-day visioning on the future of the downtown area is a good start, but what about the rest of Metro Moncton?

How we do it:

The Village of Memramcook, with citizen consultation and a consensus building approach, is in the process of long term visioning and planning, using the principles of Local Agenda 21. LA21 came to life at the World Summit on Development and the Environment at Rio de Janiero in 1992, based on the idea that many urban problems, and their solutions, have their roots in local activities. Researchers suggest focusing on 'quality of life' issues like safety, housing, economics and reducing crime which help centre the discussions on something we all are concerned about. Local Agenda 21 promotes a "participatory, long-term, strategic planning process that helps municipalities identify local sustainability priorities and implement long-term action plans. The principles are (1) that the viability-lastingness (healthiness) has to be defined locally, widely proclaimed and understood by the citizens and (2) the healthiness is linked, associated, related to the empowerment of the people and to the sharing of effective democracy at the local level. It is interesting to note that some countries attending the Rio Summit went home to involve hundreds of their local communities in the exercise of LA 21. Sweden, for example, having a history and concern for environmental politics, held consultations in all 288 Swedish communities. They then included the LA 21 in the elementary school curriculum. The World Health Organization (WHO) began a Healthy Communities Project in the 1980s which quickly flourished to a worldwide movement.

The Acadian Healthy Communities Movement (Mouvement Acadien de communautés en santé-MACSNB), headquartered in Caraquet, has been active for 10 years. Thirty-four towns and cities (from Dieppe to the Acadian Peninsula to Edmundston to Fredericton and Saint John) and a dozen community groups belong to MACSNB. Their goals are to further the concept of healthy communities and to implement a network of information, discussion and action. Presently they are working on promoting inclusion and equity (belonging and fairness) (i.e., groups like young working parents, visible minorities and newcomers, the frail, the less well-educated, the elderly) by giving presentations to their members on strategies to include these groups. Healthy Schools is their other initiative this year.

The Falls Brook Centre in Carleton County, NB is doing a series of Community Mapping meetings with people in the towns from the Tobique First Nation and Perth-Andover down the St. John River Valley to Nackawic.

These encounters bring people together to visualize "options that allow the expanding and diversification of local economy" (Falls Brook website).

Community Asset Mapping workshops invite local residents to map the assets and resources of the community from many points of view and age groups (skills, values, infrastructure, social composition, natural resources, economic services, location, history, design – the aspects outlined in this series), upon which they want to maintain and build their future. This exercise reveals many layers of good rich material and is fun besides. It is being used to identify threats (like flooding) and supports as well. Asset Mapping focuses on what we have, rather than what we need, uniting people in common purpose.

Québec City councillors created a fund for well-functioning neighbourhood associations which, upon consensus and approval of a given project, were provided some funding for it.

Does it sound like all of these aspects are beginning to run together? It should! Our aim is being able to breathe good air – and our challenge is for each of us to make some contribution to that end. Where are the community leaders who will lead the charge?

Untitled 1, Roméo Savoie, 2009

Edward Lemond

THE WONDROUS GAME

*The wondrous game that power plays with things
is to move in such submission through the world.*
Rainer Maria Rilke

Denis wondered what was going on when he came home and found the house empty. It was just after seven, not that late. Usually, Tuesday evenings, Janice would be teaching her class, and he'd scoot up the stairs to the apartment above and fix himself something to eat. He liked being alone, after spending a long day coaxing people into deals they didn't always want to make. As in a dream he'd recall a particular view of the coastline that he'd come upon or the shape of a woman's leg as she turned to go into the house that he was showing. With a smile on his face he'd step into the den where Jason might be watching TV or doing homework. He'd find Kevin, his older boy, in the living room reading a book, or in his room at the computer, though these days, ever since he had the keys to the car, he was just as likely to be at a friend's house, which for a shy boy like Kevin was a good thing, his parents believed.

Maybe one of the people taking yoga had had a heart attack and everyone had gone home. Janice sometimes asked too much of them, just as she often asked too much of herself. The mats were in place in the big downstairs room where the class met, and the lights were still on. Denis kicked off his shoes and started up the carpeted stairway. Halfway up he saw the note Janice had scribbled and left for him to see. *I tried to call you. We're at Conklin's Beach. They can't find Kevin.*

At the end of the road there were three police cars, as well as a dozen or so other cars, including Jim Beckett's, a student in the Tuesday evening class. At the entrance to the beach it was another two hundred yards to the remote corner where everyone had gathered, some close to the water, some higher up, near the boulders that formed the inroad to the breakwater. Denis cut diagonally across the beach, crunching dozens of small round pebbles with each step. He saw Jim standing with his arm around Janice's shoulder. Another man, Kevin's best friend's father, hovered near. Two police officers stood at the water's edge. One, a woman, was much shorter than the other. Everyone was looking out into the bay, where waves were forming that seemed, because of the angle of perception, higher than the land.

Denis wanted to say something as he approached, shout a word of warning so as not to frighten Janice. But she heard the sound of his foot-steps before he could think of anything. She looked at him for a moment as if she did not know who he was, and then she said, "Kevin's out there." She said it flat, as if she were reporting the passing of a cargo ship.

He saw a diver pop to the surface, and he thought his wife was suggesting that Kevin had suddenly taken up the sport of diving, dressed up in his black wet suit and mask, with an oxygen tank strapped to his back. But Kevin had never taken diving lessons. It didn't make any sense.

He shook his head and said, "What?" in a breathless voice. He looked at Jim and at Nick's father but they just stared at him and said nothing.

"They can't find him, Denis. He's gone." Jim removed his arm from around Janice's shoulder, gave Nick's father a nod, and walked with him a little ways away from the others.

The tide was rushing out, and the beach was wider and flatter, with stretches of dark brown sand. Where Janice was standing, among the pebbles, was now halfway up the beach, and she was unable to stop shivering even though she was wearing a sweatshirt and sweatpants and the blue anorak that Jim had found for her in the back of his car. It was getting dark and the policewoman wanted everyone to leave the site. But the parents would not leave until the divers came out, and so that's what they did. The divers came out, though not where the parents were standing but far away, behind the breakwater.

The Conklins and a few others who lived in nearby houses began to disperse. The police escorted the parents along the pathway through the marsh to where the cars were waiting. The policewoman went first, with a flashlight to show the path through tall grasses and weeds that were vanishing into the mist, like an army retiring for the night.

The policewoman, whose name was Sharon, followed Denis and Janice to their home and insisted on staying and keeping them company. She did not want to leave them alone. Janice was in shock, unable to speak. "We'll be all right," Denis said, but when the phone calls began to come, Janice got up and went into the kitchen where she would not have to listen. Sharon went with her and asked her if there was someone she could call to come over and stay the night. But Janice just shook her head. Sharon stood in the doorway to the kitchen, while Denis answered the phone.

Most of the calls were from friends and neighbours, encouraging Denis not to give up hope. Some wanted to know what they could do to help. "It's okay, we're doing fine," Denis said to them all. "Yes, we're still holding out hope." The fifth call was from his sister, one among the many Maritimers, brought up by the sea and in love with the sea, who had moved

52

west years ago for economic reasons. Kevin's first trip out of province had been to visit his aunt Jeanne in Calgary. He was ten at the time, and he had made several return trips. Jeanne made Denis promise to call her back, just as soon as he heard anything. "You'll be the first to know," Denis said.

The ninth call was from the woman he had been in bed with at the exact moment that his son was swept out to sea. Donna Cody had been Kevin's teacher in grade four, and the consensus was that she was the best teacher he'd ever had. She made the kids feel relaxed in her class. When she made a mistake in spelling or in addition, she would laugh at herself. She organized field trips whenever she could. She celebrated the Day of the Handicapped by asking her students to get into wheelchairs and go down-town to see how easy or difficult it was to board city buses. Everybody in Kevin's class liked Mrs. Cody, and she always said she'd never had a better group of students.

Denis usually drove the children to school, so he had more of a chance to get to know the teachers. He'd go right inside the school because he liked the feel of the place. He'd peek into the classrooms and say hello, though this was frowned upon. Because Kevin had had such a good expe-rience in Mrs. Cody's class, Denis knew that Jason was in for a treat. But the year before Jason was to enter her class her husband died suddenly of a heart attack shoveling snow. She took a leave of absence and no one saw much of her for the next few months. She was in a deep depression, by all accounts. A sister came to stay with her and then went home again.

Denis ran into her one day at the Canadian Tire store. It was June and she had come in to buy plants for her garden. He hardly recognized her, because she had dyed her hair black. When Denis suggested that the nurs-ery outside town had better plants, she said she couldn't go there because everyone knew her. She didn't want to talk to anyone, just buy some plants and go home. "You're talking to me," Denis said. And there was something in the way he looked at her that made her laugh. She couldn't remember the last time she had laughed.

What Denis offered her was not sympathy but friendship. He never talked about Mike, her husband, and never asked her if she still thought about him all the time. He just assumed she did. He talked about the garden, about books they were both reading, about movies, trips they had taken or might take in the future. He made her believe that she did have a future – and a present. Even if sometimes it seemed like a pretty paltry thing. "I wish we'd had a child together," she said once, and Denis didn't realize until later that she was talking about her dead husband, not him.

With her interest in meditation, yoga, and veganism, Janice had veered off in ways that were completely unexpected and, to Denis, unwelcome. He separated from her emotionally. She needed and wanted his friendship less and less. And so he gave it to Donna. He never stopped loving his wife, or telling himself that he loved his wife, but they were bored with each other. He began to find faults in her that he had never seen before, such as legs that were too thick. He would sometimes say to himself, Who is this strange woman in bed next to me? He felt he was alone again, as he had been alone during his teenage years and into his twenties, when he met Janice and she seemed really to want to listen to what he had to say. Before he met Janice he had always thought that he had to force himself on others, if he wanted to get them to listen.

There were more phone calls, until finally Denis said enough is enough and unplugged the phone. It was midnight, and the only person asleep was Jason, on the couch in the den. Sharon, the policewoman, had left, after Janice, with a nod of her head, insisted that she was going to be okay. But Janice was not okay. She sat at the table in the kitchen, mute as unfinished plaster. Denis wanted to say something but did not know how to begin. Somewhere she had found a pack of cigarettes and she stayed up all night smoking one after the other, something she had not done in years. Denis sat on the couch in the living room looking at the glass doors that opened onto the back veranda, wanting to believe that Kevin might walk in at any moment. Instead, he saw his own reflection.

The bodies washed up on shore in the morning, and the parents were asked to identify them. It was a big news story in all the papers as far away as Moncton and Halifax, and on the radio. There was even a mention in one of the Toronto papers. Donna was listening to the local news when she heard that the bodies had been found. She picked up the phone and called Denis on his cell phone. He was in the car with Janice on his way to identify the body of his son. Without having thought it through, he said the first thing that came to mind, "I can't see you anymore." The words shook Janice from her zombie state and she looked at him and then she looked away again, returning to her private world, which was not a world of thoughts or images but of vague or sometimes powerful feelings that swept over her like the rising and falling of the tide.

After driving Janice home again Denis went in search of a copy of the local newspaper because he wanted to know what was being said. It was Wednesday and normally there would be plenty of copies in the stores, but today it was all sold out. The clerk in one of the stores said, "Nothing sells like a drowning, unless it's a crash." Denis looked him in the eye and said, "I'm the father of one of those boys who died." The clerk just shrugged and said, "I'm sorry," and Denis walked out.

He drove out of town, thinking that in one of the convenience stores up the coast there'd be a copy. He lost his FM classical music station along the way, so he switched to the local news where the accident was still being discussed, as it had been all morning. The news that the bodies had been found had contributed a note of finality that allowed a new level of speculation and analysis. One of the reporters, relying on police sources, attempted to reconstruct the sequence of events. Nick and Kevin and two girls had gone to the beach for a swim. A sign warned that the beach was closed because of strong undercurrents. The boys, however, decided to try it anyway. One of the girls, Sophie, had dared them and therefore they had to do it.

A political commentator, so-called, attempted to address the question of who was responsible. The more he listened the angrier Denis became. He stopped the car by the side of the road and called the station and said he wanted to be interviewed. It took them a moment to understand who he was. "Are you sure you want to do this?" the voice at the other end said. "I need to set some things straight," Denis said.

The interview was scheduled later in the day, during a phone-in show. Denis agreed to speak first, so that callers would have a chance to respond to his comments. By the time he entered the studio his anger had subsided. All he wanted people to understand was that these were good kids. It had been a colossal 'error of judgment,' he could agree to that. Young people sometimes do stupid things, like all people do, and you cannot really blame them. They take risks. It's part of growing up. The police will have to know who did what and why and when, but for the parents it did not matter which boy went in first and who or what made him do it. They did not want to know. It was a terrible accident. Just that. Nothing more.

Denis couldn't stop thinking about the girls who had witnessed the accident. They were there and they saw what happened. They had to go through the whole process, telling the story again and again while hardly able to believe it themselves. He wanted to see how they were. The girls' parents, however, discouraged him from visiting. It would not be a good idea just yet. The girls were too shaken up.

But a few days later, at the farmer's market, he saw Sophie with her parents. They had finished their shopping and were walking to their car, lugging bags of fresh produce. Sophie was Kevin's girlfriend. She was a short girl, with green eyes and freckles, and she had long ago decided she was not going to be ashamed of anything she said or did. If a boy didn't like her because she was too outspoken, she'd find another boy. Kevin was the third boy she'd taken up with this year but she liked him the best. Whenever she tried to provoke him he'd just smile back, disarming her.

When she saw Denis, Sophie broke away from her parents and made her way back through the crowd of people to where he was waiting.

She had not heard his interview on the radio but she had read about it in the paper the next day. "I just wanted to tell you, Mr. Martin, how brave I think you are, because you spoke out the way you did. You weren't even thinking about yourself, you were thinking about us. That's so generous. I cry when I think about it."

Her words almost knocked him down, and he grabbed hold of the table where he was standing, which happened to be Jim Beckett's table where he sold fresh eggs. "This is all new to me, Sophie. I'm just feeling my way here. I try to be true to who I am, even if I fail most of the time."

"I've got to go now," Sophie said, and she gave him a hug.

Donna was waiting in the parking lot. She was standing by her car, in a long flowery dress. Denis looked at her, and he did not know if he should go to her or not. Finally, he got into his own car and drove away.

This Close to Me

A man in a bathing cap bobbed in the water a hundred yards from shore, oblivious to the light rain that was falling. In the distance, where the beach ended at an outcropping of rock, a man was playing with his dog, running with him and throwing sticks into the water for him to chase. Adele began walking along the beach in the opposite direction, away from the man with his dog and away from the lone swimmer. The day was unusually warm and muggy. There was no wind. The water was calm. Three or four sailboats drifted under gray skies a mile or so from shore. Toward the head of the bay an island, dull green in the mist, called to her.

She took off her shoes and socks and left them on the beach at the foot of a lifeguard's twelve-foot-high chair. Near the water the sand was smooth and hard-packed, while higher up it was rough, uneven, like ground ploughed by drunken oxen. Adele preferred the rough, deep-furrowed sand. It made her work; it made her breathe; it made her think. She had trouble keeping her balance, and every few steps she'd fall and get up again. There were people watching her from the deck of a restaurant built much too near the sand dunes but she did not care. She wasn't drunk but she felt drunk. She began running, making noises deep in her throat of the sort that a person shoveling snow or climbing a mountain might make. When she stepped on a shell or a fragment of a shell she'd wince and go on, ascending and descending the beach, she couldn't be sure.

She ran almost a mile before the beach slid off into mud and then a wide lagoon, which smelled of seaweed, dead shell fish, and gasoline exhaust. Her heart was thumping and she was breathing in through her mouth, trying to fight off the smells. Straight ahead, across the lagoon, was a wharf with its protected marina. People walked back and forth on the wharf. To the left, along the shoreline, were a few houses that marked the extreme boundary of the town. Seagulls squawked lazily over the lagoon, as if they were unenthusiastic stand-ins. Crows called from the tops of the houses and from the trees behind the houses. A sailboat moved out from the marina, in a direction that would take it between the island and the beach, but nearer the island.

She began walking toward the island. The water was no more than ankle deep. She kept walking and walking and the water was never more than ankle deep. Even very far out there were still sandbars that she could stand on and feel the water wash over her feet. She stopped at one of the sandbars and looked back at the distance she had come. There were a few people now on the beach, near the roped-in area. The lifeguard was sitting on her perch. Adele spoke Janice's name aloud, to the seagulls that were flying near, to the crows that she could still see hovering near the houses, and, turning once more, to the animals on the island, as if explaining to them why she was here. My daughter Janice died. We laughed together. We were always in each other's thoughts, encouraging when one was discouraged or afraid or didn't understand. She was this close to me. She held her hands together to describe this closeness. She wished her daughter could see the same horizon, hear the same sounds, share in the same delights. But suddenly the silence was deeper than before, the birds all disappeared, and she sank to her knees on the sandbar. She waited for the tears to come.

The sun broke through the gray of the sky, then disappeared again, as if some other form of gravity were sucking it back. Adele remembered the same shade of gray when Janice was born, when she first emerged. She's dead, Adele thought, surprised to find herself so calm in the face of catastrophe. She did not cry the way babies usually cry. She did not move or even open her eyes. Life – or death – is unfolding, as it should, Adele said to herself. She was not in charge. But the doctor did something to the baby's mouth or tongue, even as she was hanging there upside down, as gray and slimy as a fish, and when she screamed Adele knew that everything was not lost.

"Still Life With Mother And Child," Adele titled her next painting. She worked with cut-out figures and spray paint because she had so little time and she needed a method that would give her much quicker results between feedings and changing of the diapers. The child had no features and looked dead, she couldn't help it. The colors, though, were bright primary colors, so that the immediate impression was one of joy – glad tidings. Somebody told her that Matisse had worked in a similar way toward the end of his life when he began to go blind. But Adele said, "I'm not going blind, I'm pressed for time."

She did a series of works on the theme of mother and child, all using the same technique – large collages of colored paper cut-outs. She used spray paint to color the paper even though friends urged her not to, saying that spray paint was bad for her health, especially as a mother who was nursing her child. But she wanted quick results, and she was in no mood to listen to advice, friendly or not, that would thwart her ambition. Everyone agreed that the works were good enough to be shown. Adele went to the Mary Boone Gallery, which had recently opened on West Broadway, but Mary Boone was not interested. She was kind enough, though, to put her in contact with a woman named Cindy Nemser, a feminist art critic and advocate for women artists. Nemser pointed Adele in the direction of the A.I.R. gallery on Wooster Street in Brooklyn, not far from the artists' co-op where Adele had her own studio. Adele was thrilled to be invited to exhibit at this gallery, which was the first and most important artist-run space for women artists in the United States. Her name would be out there. Somebody would write a review. Her career, just possibly, would take off. Adele, however, was the last to see what others saw immediately, that the child in the collages was unreal, dead, grotesque, and the mother was blind, unable to see that she was holding and nurturing what was already beyond revival. All along she had been denying the obvious, until someone pointed it out to her. Then she turned against her own project. She felt that she was being pushed into something, an advocate for radical feminism, that she did not really much like. Her ambitions proved stillborn, like the child in the collages. Ten years later, when she gave up painting, she destroyed all her collages, along with many other works she had done during those years.

A motor boat appeared in the periphery of her vision, coming toward her from the direction of the wharf. She had moved out into the water to the point where it was about knee deep. She was wearing a white shirt and she was quite visible, she thought. She waved but the boat kept coming, as if on a dare. Suddenly afraid, she retreated to the sandbar she had just vacated. The boat came within a few feet of her, even though the water was shallow. The young couple waved as if it were the most normal thing they were doing and to them it probably was. But they had frightened Adele and she had trouble catching her breath. She remained on the sandbar for long minutes, as waves of anger washed over her. The motor boat, bouncing on the water, ventured farther out and eventually disappeared in the middle of the bay. Only the smell of its exhaust lingered, until finally this too was carried into the upper atmosphere.

She heard the voices of the children playing in the water in the roped-off area, under the watchful eye of the lifeguard. She heard the call of a loon from somewhere near the tip of the island. A light rain was falling. She spoke Janice's name again, softly. Something deep in her chest was loosened. The coolness of the water and the fact that she was alone, completely alone, with only the sound of the children playing, created a strange feeling of exhilaration. She began to beat herself on the chest with her doubled-up fists, one fist hitting over the heart, lightly at first and then hard, the other hitting into the solar plexus. Instead of breathing she was knocking the breath out of herself. She kept hitting herself and calling the name, as if she expected to see Janice just ahead in the water, floating on her back, or standing on the shore of the island in white flowing robes, waving. I've cried for you, daughter, and I thought I was done crying. But here I am again. Only it's not me crying. It's the trees, the water, the birds, the houses, everything around me. The children.

The tide had gone out, leaving the sandbar more visible and solid than before. The rain felt soft and warm on the skin, almost a mist. She removed her clothes and left them on the sandbar, folded neatly at the highest level. As she waded up to her waist and began vigorously shivering, a taste of salt on her lips, she realized that she had not come here, to the shelf of the continent, to be blown away by speed boats or high winds or rain or deranged men. And with this resolve, and her arms beginning to resist the float to the middle of nowhere, she took the plunge and swam towards the island, towards whatever might lay ahead.

Shape-Shifter

Within the first ten feet the path has turned soft and muddy, marking the beginning of the bog where I know I can escape. Where it is very soggy someone has placed logs to be used as steppingstones. Where the water is ankle deep I avoid the path altogether, seeking out root systems of near-by trees, clinging to the trees when I have to, to keep my balance. Even if she wanted to follow me into the woods, there's no way the caretaker can negotiate the path I've chosen.

It is my 70th birthday, and I wanted to go walking before supper. Nothing else interested me, and why should it after being kept inside for days and weeks. I said it would be just like the old days, when I made lists of birds and she gathered fallen leaves to press in her book. She uses these leaves in her artwork. She rehabilitates nature.

I was patient, waiting for my chance. Let her walk ahead, I said to myself. Let her find a leaf that she can't do without.

And when she bent down to retrieve it I simply vanished.

Shape-shifter she is fond of calling me, because I am forever disappearing at parties, or art openings, or shopping malls. One second I am there, the next I am gone. I don't like to stand around and do nothing. A salmon that's not moving is dead, my father taught me.

Since the park is within the city limits, she thought nothing much could happen.

She is so easily deceived.

I can hear her calling my name but I don't answer. A minute has passed, no more. I've gone off to take a leak, she probably thinks. I do it all the time. She's waiting for me to come galumphing out of the woods, like Banquo's ghost.

Let her wait.

I've come to an odd construction deep in the woods. Narrow planks are nailed to big plastic tubing, the kind used to carry sewage away from beachfront properties, or to funnel water in drainage ditches under a road.

The trick is to keep my balance while moving steadily ahead.

The sooner I stop hearing the hysterical voice the better.

These planks are like the ever-shrinking threads linking one part of my brain to the other, twisting through thickets of decay. I've seen the future, in shades of grey, and it's not pretty.

She's beginning to realize I'm not coming back. I can hear the panic in her voice, which grows louder even as I move farther away.

She'll stop a passer-by and ask to use his cell phone to call the police. When that happens I know I won't have much time before they come looking for me. They'll find volunteers to help in the search, people who never gave a shit about me when I was sitting in the window losing my mind.

I come to the end of the planking and step down into the soggy earth. The trees are black, stripped bare, and coated with something mucous that glistens in the fading light. There's a smell of rotting vegetation.

I find myself standing by the side of a road. One way, to my right, leads into town with its bright lights. The other way leads into the country-side, which is already shrouded in darkness. I look one way, then the other.

A car stops and the couple inside ask if I want a ride. I look at the woman, then the man. The man taps the steering wheel. "Get in," the woman says. "You'll catch your death."

"I'm taking the low road," I tell them.

The woman wants to say something, perhaps inquire as to my intentions. Before she has a chance, the man drives on.

I walk along the road toward the woods. The wind blows right through my coat. It's cold.

I keep walking, until I come to a tunnel under the high road. I've been waiting for her to have a change of heart. Keep your head down, I told myself. Don't push things. She'll come around. But it's been five years. What's the point of waiting another five years?

Overhead, the traffic is a low, steady hum.

If it's dark on the road, it's darker still in the woods.

Crows, even at this late hour, notice and protest my arrival. I hear their calls and I feel the flutter of their wings in the trees.

I come to some sort of gate at the edge of the forest, and I push it open. My hand feels numb. I shake it as I was taught – in tai chi.

I am alone, yet not alone. The crows, in making a loud show of their displeasure, are my companions.

Under a tree at the edge of the forest, on a bed of leaves, not far from the gate that I opened, I find a place to lie down.

I am sheltered from the rain.

Night is falling, and I have no names to call it.

I have trouble sleeping because of a pain in my shoulder. I must have slipped and fallen but I cannot remember where or when.

Must it always be so?

I sit against the trunk of the tree but sleep, in this position, is at best fitful. My head rolls, falls, and snaps back.

I'm torn between sleep and wakefulness. Asleep, I drift and float. Awake, I see things that I never thought I would see.

Creatures appear in the dark with phosphorescent eyes brought on by rain. Monstrous birds perch on the limbs of trees, and when they call out the ground trembles.

I try to move my arms but they've gone numb and will not move. Every effort only adds to paralysis.

In a dream I'm standing in a mountain gorge and a rockslide falls on me. I'm no more than an insect under it. Then a solitary man appears and pulls me out from under the rubble. He gives me water and I feel released.

There is a light filtering through the trees.

Crows call from far away.

The cat-like complaint I hear is the wheezing deep in my lungs.

I'm cold.

Dawn brings a new day. When will it end?

All around me there is only – silence.

If it is all I have left now – the silence – I will keep it – keep it alive.

Something Happened
(For A. L.)

You wanted to be where it was happening, where
great events would change the course of history and
nothing would ever be the same. You were in
Montreal, for instance, when it looked like the
country was about to tear itself apart – you
wanted to see what that would be like. Later, when
you were living in Vancouver, you crossed the border in
buses to see just how ugly Seattle could get, with
props in place, cameras rolling, and the
whole world watching. When I was your age and I
wanted everything turned upside down, I'd
go away for a while, or I'd change careers, or I'd meet some
one new, or somebody would die … it was all so much easier.

We get thrown into the world, say the philosophers, and
if this is true, you made the best of a bad situation, by
throwing yourself at events – as observer, participant, and
(later) reporter. Even before you knew you wanted to be a
journalist, you had the instincts of a journalist, the
same way that a future film-maker might walk a
way from her friends, toward the end of the beach, rather than
stay and listen to some boy telling dirty jokes around the fire.

It seemed only natural, in the spring of 2001, just after
university, that you would choose New York City, be
cause New York City was where the next big thing was most like
ly to happen. What you hadn't counted on was being so close by when
it did happen, and you had not imagined that it would take the
form that it did. Exiting your office at the Village Voice, and
turning north to escape the smoke and the flames, you
felt rather than saw the first building fall, and if
I can quote you here, from something that
you wrote a few days later, incomprehensible
thunder cracked inside you and shook the
screams of thousands now clogging the streets.

Something happened that I don't yet
understand. Even several years after the event you

don't want to see me, or talk to me. It's as if when those
workers trapped on the upper floors threw themselves from the
windows, you threw yourself into a new way of looking at
things and you subsequently found it impossible or
unseemly to share this with me. Walking away from the
stricken towers, you were also walking away from me.

Les Pierres de Paris, Elaine Amyot, 1990

Elaine Amyot

GATE FIVE
(An Excerpt from "The Seven Gates" – a Memoir)

With Raymond as guide I am able to go deeper into dreams and into childhood memories. I am able to re-experience past events, to do collages of them, and to let them go.

In one of the sessions I am at my mother's knee. I am very young, perhaps three. We live on Tâché Street, before my brother's birth. We are at a neighbour's – Mrs. Hogg. It is a Ladies' aide meeting. We have delicious thin salmon and celery sandwiches. The crusts have been cut off. My mother sits there, not speaking. I can feel her fear. I do not know how to help her. I remain still. I eat the sandwich. I look at the curtain of small brass beads that covers the doorway to the kitchen.

Once home, after this session with Raymond, the collage I do is with torn paper except for the figure of the mother. I cut her out of brown paper. She has a crown of thorns, an X over her bosom, hiding her green, red heart. A cord leads from her to me, a small child. Over my heart is a black sack – not mine, tied to the brown link of a cord to the mother.

*

When I was ten my mother could not understand why I had such difficulty in getting to sleep. I couldn't tell her about the man. To talk about him would be to admit that he frightened me and I wanted him out of my dream world. He came silently. I never saw his face, for before I could turn around and open my eyes he had slipped a sack over my head. It was a pillow case, which he tied around my throat with a rope. Holding this he would lead me off the bed, into the living room, out of the house and throughout our town. In the morning I would wake up tired but relieved to be able to breathe freely once more.

*

The year was 1942. These were dark times.
THE WAR.

*

Charles, my favourite uncle, had been living with us, but with the war he had joined the RCAF and was reported 'missing in action.' Every evening we listened to war news. Charles was a rear gunner in a Lancaster – we knew that this was very dangerous but not knowing where he was flying made us even more anxious. We would not talk about this, but we were aware of the destruction and pain people overseas were experiencing.

The sense of doom, of a heavy black cloud covering what was beautiful and natural, was present, especially at bed time. My bedroom was not a comfort. It was cold – we had no central heating and there were no rugs on the floors. The metal bed had squeaky bed springs, a thin mattress and the only blanket was from the first world war – an army issue woollen blanket, slate coloured with a grey stripe. Armies must have used these in the time of the Boer War and perhaps they are still in use in Afghanistan today. I did not feel brave and for diversion I would imagine that the little holes in the green window blind were star constellations to which I gave names.

*

At the time of my divorce I had a dream that had some similarities with the recurring dreams of my pubescence. This dream was also very intense – it is still vivid and real today, thirty-four years later.

The Dream

I am going up a stairway and I am looking into a grey cube of a room. In its center is a brass bed, its head a curved delicate gold. Seated in the middle of this are three large dolls – girl-woman dolls. They sit back to back, each pointing to a different direction. Their dolls' articulated limbs do not move. Over each head is a cloth sack, tied at the throat by a thick cord. I am transfixed by these hooded heads for although the covering seems to be of a heavy cloth, through this tissue can be seen huge black cavities where eyes should be, cavities similar to the black eye cavities in skulls. I have read since that they are archetypal eyes of death – profound, implacable, like the eyes in the skulls around the house of the Russian goddess-witch Baba Yaga. They see beyond illusions and defences. They see not what might be good or bad but an unmasked reality.

The bed spread is black with a design of red cherries, yellow and white daisies and green leaves. Their colour is so intense that it vibrates. It is part of me. I resonate and not only do I see and feel but I hear sound – something harmonious, penetrating, beautiful.

For several years after this I try to capture that experience. I make a small painting, in oil pastels. I try to do drawings of it, paintings sculptures. But each effort seems so weak compared to the actual event that I am discouraged but I continue to try.

The image of a doll woman, her head covered by a sack, her eye cavities black, persists in my work. She stops appearing after I make three small girl-dolls with sacks over their heads, rope around their necks, and hang them from a nail in the wall.

During this time, in sessions with Raymond, I am able to revisit my childhood. I am able to recall a time of innocence and a time of lost innocence. The first incident that clearly made me aware that we were different took place in the spring of 1938. I had just turned six. My father was sitting in his big rocking chair and I was sitting on his lap.

CHILDHOOD MEMORIES:

STARTING SCHOOL

This chair was no ordinary piece of furniture. It held a place of importance in our large living-and-dining-room. It sat apart from the rest of the furniture and was the focus for entertainment until the arrival of a new gleaming streamlined floor model radio three years later. For now, it was a warm presence that recalled pleasant moments and promised the possibility of many more. Its black leather covering was held in place by bright brass tacks that were shaped like miniature volcanoes and that tasted cold and sour on my tongue. It had large flat wooden arms, unvarnished and discoloured where generations of hands had rested or pounded. It was easy to imagine that from this chair, gossip had been shared, problems had been solved, private moments of anguish had been rocked away, stories passed on and many songs sung.

My father continued the tradition and told us tales of "Ti-Jean" and "des Loups garou." He recited Victor Hugo's "La Chanson de Roland" and sang what he called a pot-pourri of French songs – some of which I would eventually teach to young school children.

This chair was wide enough for my brother and I to sit back to back. With feet firmly planted on the rockers and hands gripping the wide arms, we rocked happily back and forth singing with gusto "Jésus mon fort et mon rocher" (our favourite hymn taught us by Grandmère Brunet), or the songs so much loved by our father. Our mother, to my knowledge, never sat in that chair. But then, Mother did not sing – not ever.

Now that I was six I was telling my father how eager I was to go to school in the fall. Eager because I would be going with my best friend Georgette. She already was prepared and had her long-sleeved black dress with its pleated skirt, her white celluloid collar and cuffs, her long black stocking and her black shoes. Georgette was my very best friend – in fact, my only friend. When I had trouble getting to sleep, my mother would tell me to think of good things. My thoughts would be of rosy apples, pale green and pink, and of Georgette. She lived two doors away over her grandfather's general store, where we sampled the candies – little wax bottles filled with sweet red liquid and my favourite, flat pink and white marshmallow circles which had in the centre a little chocolate man. Georgette's mother Bertha Boucher and my mother were close friends. They had little in common with their neighbours who had numerous children, who were devout, practicing Roman Catholics and who were part of large family living nearby. There was little or no communication with them.

When I told my father that not only was I looking forward to going to school with Georgette but I was eager to have my black dress and stockings, he said, in his big stern voice (the voice of thunder, the voice that meant that it was useless to protest), "No, you are not going to L'école La Joie, you are going to a different school." I was numb with shock, struck dumb by this unbelievable news – unbelievable because Georgette and I were inseparable.

I do not recall any further talk about school that spring. My parents never referred to it and since I did not want to open a forbidden, dangerous topic, neither did I. During the two summer months, when as usual I was sent to the Eastern townships to my aunt Amabelle, her three daughters, older than I, patiently, but with much laughter taught me to say in English, Yes, No, and May I have a glass of water please. Thus I was prepared to enter Grade one at the Joliette Intermediate School in September, 1938.

GRADE ONE, JOLIETTE INTERMEDIATE SCHOOL (PROTESTANT) SEPTEMBER, 1938

I don't remember how or with whom I got to school that first day. What I do remember is sitting at a desk, barely conscious of my surroundings. I did not dare to turn around or to look to my left where I knew there were rows of desks, inhabited by a large mass, and beyond this – the unknown. The desks were of highly varnished wood, resting on ornate wrought iron supports and bolted, not to the floor but to long narrow lengths of wood. This arrangement made it possible to move 5 desks, a row, at a time, to prepare for concerts, rummage sales or games.

My own desk had layers of varnish which gave it a look of taffy – the 'tire" that my mother made every November 25th on "la fête de la Ste Catherine," la sainte des vieilles filles. I focused on this desk top for most of the day, and after the initial time of semi-consciousness, I began to examine the many markings carved in its surface. These were strange and interesting. Who had made them? When? Most importantly, what did they mean? They were tangible evidence that I was not alone in my suffering, that others had been here in this very place. I was suffering, but in silence. With a shake of my head my long ringlets would fall on either side of my face making me feel protected. Not being able to see others I fancied that I could not be seen. It was a comfort to not see others seeing me. I could not understand what was happening around me. There was movement and sound, I was immersed in it but remained untouched – nothing penetrated. I felt vulnerable and unprotected and sensed danger. I wished that I had a box around me, a box like a telephone booth, with a window in the front and buttons to push to prevent sound from coming in. This would shield me from the meaningless noise of words that filled the air around me.

I was wearing a new dress, made by my mother for this occasion. It was of pale pink cotton organdy with an overall pattern of roses and pale green leaves, trimmed with emerald green rick-rack. It was a sundress, square-necked and sleeveless but with a little matching bolero, a style common in the thirties. Around my neck, on a very long chain, hung a large gold-coloured locket, not appropriate for school but since it was a gift from my father I had wanted to wear it. It would touch the desk when I leant forward and made a concrete connection between what was real and now, that is, Father, home, French, and what was new and frightening in this moment. And by far the most fearsome aspect of this day was the presence of our teacher, Mrs. Copping. She wanted to leave no doubt that she was in charge, and so from her chair behind the solid desk on a platform high above us she barked out her orders. When she stood she seemed so very tall to me. Her height was emphasized by the long vertical row of buttons, bells, that began at her high neckline and ended inches from the floor at her hem. Her hands fascinated me – they were like wax, the skin transparent over her very long thin fingers. She would insert her little finger in one ear and move it very quickly up and down, a sight that never failed to amaze me. Four years later, after my brother had begun school, he, the engineer-to-be, took apart an alarm clock exposing its bell and its metal arms. When we saw the rapid motion of the arm against the bell we both exclaimed with surprised recognition: "Madame Copping!"

On this first day I did not take in my surroundings, nor could I distinguish students – they were part of a mass of moving, squirming entities. At some point in this very long first day I heard my name spoken in a clear, penetrating shrill "Elaine!" When I looked up, I heard "Stand up!" and understood that this meant for me to do as the others were doing. Then when others sat, I sat. It became a game, to be alert and to do what the others were doing. So the day passed – standing, sitting, sitting, sitting, and standing. A bell was rung. It was a hand bell rung by a designated student from the upper grades. School was over, and I was the last to leave.

MY BROTHER EDWARD THOMAS

Mother made sure that we knew his name was Edward – pronounced à la English and not the French "Edouard." Her mother, a Swiss protestant whose main language was French nevertheless did not want to be associated with French Canadians who were 99% Roman Catholic and considered by her family to be an inferior race. Mother lived this prejudice which must have caused her difficulties because my father, although Protestant, was a "pure laine" Québecois. Grandmother tolerated him because of his religion but she never let an opportunity pass without correcting his French. With a bland expression seen only in her presence he would refer to "Holiette" (Joliette), "deuce" (deux), "pétraves" (betteraves) and would ask her to "dé-greyez-vous" (literally, unrig yourself). She never failed to react immediately and showed no interest in the origins of these Québecois expressions.

At home, Edward was called "Gars-Gars" (pronounced Gaw-Gaw) or "Ti-Gars" or, only by my mother, "Mon beau "ptit bébé bleu" crooned in a voice trembling with emotion. I was "la "ptite" or, for some reason known only to my mother, "la drine." This title always made me feel ashamed and humiliated, for if there was warmth in the tone used to refer to me as "la drine" I did not feel it. It made me feel apart, different, not quite human. I was able to keep it secret at school until one fateful day in Grade six, when all 32 children of our school were pounding up the stairs at recess, shouting "La drine, la drine." My mischievous little brother was responsible. After this "La drine" was never mentioned again. It was no longer a family secret. I had been humiliated enough. Episode closed.

My first glimpse of Edward was early in the morning of February 22nd, 1936. He had just been born. As was the custom then, babies were born at home and siblings were sent to a neighbour's during the birthing. I do not remember where I had spent the night but I do recall vividly being brought in to my parents' bedroom early that dark morning. This was a place where I was never permitted to enter. My mother was in bed. I had never seen her in bed. Her long auburn hair was not in its usual bun but was free, covering her shoulders with its shimmering copper and gold. It looked so alive that I wanted to touch it.

Beside her was something new – a bundle of sky blue cloth. I was told that this was 'mon "ptit frère." There had been no mention of his expected arrival, no preparation. Being only three years and ten months old I accepted without surprise whatever the adults presented ... so ... I had a little brother.

The most wonderful thing about this event for me was not the arrival of a new baby but the fact that this baby was complete. When Mother drew back the soft blue wrap she exposed his tiny hands and I was transfixed – he had delicate, pink, perfect miniature fingernails. A marvel.

Later that day my best friend Georgette, who lived two doors down the street from us, was also presented with a baby brother, Bernard. Bernard was skinny and pale, with dry, scaly skin, whereas Edward, who weighed ten pounds, had pink skin, blue eyes, and blond hair. Such colouration was rare in French Canada and therefore considered special. We accepted Edward but did not talk about Bernard.

Georgette and I were told by my father that it was Indians who had brought us the babies. I imagined an Indian wearing a huge feathered headdress like the one on the cover of one of my storybooks. He would be carrying a large brown sack over his shoulder, as did Santa Claus or le Bonhomme Sept Heures. (Bonhomme Sept Heures put any child who was not in bed by seven o'clock into his sack.) I thought that the Indian must have been kept very busy bringing babies to houses and collecting children. Where he brought them was a mystery. There were many new babies on our street but I never noticed if any children disappeared. I didn't want to know.

My early memories of "mon frère" are many and varied, in the same way that his adventures were many and varied. He had a large head (we French Canadians called these "des têtes carrées" (square heads), fine blondish hair, a lisp (he couldn't say words with "r" until he began school), and eyes that my mother said were like the sea, at times a grey-green, other times smoky-blue. When he was excited they became black.

They were black the day he came running breathless into the kitchen, his singed eyebrows giving his face a new look, imploring Mother "Dis-le pas à Papa" (Don't tell Papa). He'd taken Father's corn pipe, and he and Marcel, his friend from next door, had tried to smoke shredded Montreal Herald paper.

They were black when he was gripped by his obsession for plugging openings with whatever was at hand – nails, screws, blocks of wood. Mother had a hard time removing a swollen wood block he'd stuck in the drain hole of her new wringer washing machine. She was never able to remove a large screw stuck in the silver fuel holder of a silver heirloom egg cooker. It is still there.

I admired his courage. He liked to try new things. For example, one day when he was three he had been unusually quiet. Mother should have checked up on him but she hadn't. He had taken Father's drill brace and bit, a tool almost as tall as himself, and had successfully drilled a hole in the front room floor. This was a room that was used only when my parents sang and played the large table piano. When Mother saw the hole her lips became a tight line – something we grew to dread. She said the classic "attend que ton père arrive" (wait until your father gets here). When Father entered the house and saw, in the room next to the hall, Mother, me, and the culprit around the hole in the floor, his colour changed to bright red. I thought that he would roar – he had a very big voice, like thunder, frightening.

Before he could do this, my brother, who had been balancing from one foot to the other, arms behind his back (a pose copied from Father), said, in a calm, serious voice, the voice of one adult speaking to another, "Ça prend un Christ de fou pour faire ça, eh Papa?" ("It takes one hell of a fool to do such a thing, eh Father?")

In my family it is my brother who is noticed. He is blond, blue-eyed, charming, courageous, and very intelligent. I am the obverse – silent, admiring, invisible. I am alone, separate, lost, without identity. The Savignac incident has left me with a terrible legacy, exacerbated because I have no one to talk to. I have no voice.

LES PIERRES DE PARIS

The necklace was kept in a special box in my parents' bedroom. The room had double doors that were paneled in rose-coloured glass, glass that was smooth on one side but patterned with ridges on the other. The ridges radiated from centres so that the panels seemed to be covered with stars. When my parents were at home, I was not allowed into this room. When they were away, it was understood that I might go in. I never entered the room immediately, but savoured the moment by pressing my face against the glass and looking into a room filled with slivers of pink light where familiar objects were transformed into mysterious shapes.

The special box that held the necklace was in the left-hand drawer of Mother's small vanity table. The table had an oval mirror and a recessed middle section flanked by two vertical drawers. Mother, who did not wear make-up, never used it for its intended purpose. When she brushed her long auburn hair, she never looked into the mirror but would coil it into a bun and pierce it fiercely with a hair pin that she had grimly held in her mouth. She always did things quickly, as if the present moment was not as important as what was to be done next.

The vanity table was used to hold the things that were precious and sacred to her. The ritual of touching these objects was done slowly and because they were always kept in the same places I could anticipate with pleasure the discovery of the familiar. Her Bible, which she kept nearest the bed, I usually opened first, for I liked the feel of the thin, delicate pages, edged in red gold, and wondered at their transparent strength. I would study the sixteen coloured illustrations, always saving my favourite for the last, an Arab beside the river Jordan. The scenery was pale and flat, but the colour of his long garment, a deep mauve, always made me catch my breath.

Other objects she kept in boxes in the vertical drawers. They were not just ornaments I was touching but links to stories of my mother's family, of events that happened long ago and in distant places. From a small blue box I would take out the delicate gold and tourquoise pendant, imagining my mother's oncle Frédérick stumbling through the rubble of the San Fransisco earthquake, picking up this trinket and years later giving it to my mother, a small girl. I was particularly fond of holding a small booklet that was covered with diamond-shaped pieces of mother-of-pearl that radiated soft hues of the rainbow. It had linen pages that kept sewing needles used many years ago by my great grandmother. The inscription in the central diamond-shaped piece, done in an elegant, very fine script, spelt "Souvenir de Bertha."

I always saved until last the box with the necklace of blue stones. It was of honey-coloured wood, long and narrow, with an unusual lid that, when opened, stayed attached to the box by two curious iron mechanisms, permitting the lid to stay behind the box and thus allowing a full view of the contents. The necklace belonged to La belle Bertha de Berne, my Swiss great grandmother. Before her marriage she had had a personal maid to do her hair but after coming to Namur, Quebec with her pastor husband, she had led a very different life – not one that she was used to. A relative of hers returning from Paris had brought her a necklace of blue stones, known in our family as "Les pierres de Paris." The stones were spheres, the colour of summer twilight, a soft blue that held shades of green. No two spheres were exactly alike. Looking into their smoky depths I would see magical worlds of intimate immensity.

A difficult landlord caused my father to decide to move. Our new place was on la rue Notre Dame. There, with no pink glass doors to create a world of magic, I made no more visits to Mother's vanity table. It seemed that I was shut out of her world of objects with their stories. But then one day she created a bridge to her world by offering me "Les pierres de Paris," saying I was now old enough to wear them. Wearing the necklace gave me a feeling of pride and excitement, for I felt that what I was entering into now was new territory.

On the way to school that first morning of wearing the necklace, I was followed by a boy on a bicycle. This boy had been following me for several days, riding very slowly, sometimes stopping, sometimes coming near and trying to get my attention by talking. I knew that he went to the Roman Catholic school, l'école St. Viateur, and not the Protestant school I attended, Joliette Intermediate School. When he tried talking to me, I pretended to be indifferent. I felt vulnerable and afraid that he would turn out to be someone who would mock me and call me "une maudite protestante" – words I had heard often enough that I dreaded them. In my anxiety I clutched at the necklace, and it broke – its blue stones scattering on grass and pavement. I was rigid with shock, but the boy quickly left his bicycle, knelt on his hands and knees and began picking up the stones. I was crying, making it difficult for me to find any of the stones. The boy found them all, even the small ones, and placed them in my hand. We did not talk or look at each other but I felt his nearness. When he placed the stones in my hand, a small pleasant shock of warmth spread from his hand to mine. I was not conscious of the time it took us to gather the stones, but we collected all of "Les pierres de Paris."

That afternoon when I came home from school with the broken necklace I wanted so much to speak to my mother about my feelings. I had glimpsed a new world, one that was still strange to me, but that I was closer to knowing.

KETTLE DRUMS

The New Brunswick symphony is playing at a concert at the Capitol Theatre in Moncton. Much to my delight there is a percussion section. I look at the kettledrums and I am transported to another time.

It is Montréal, la rue Jeanne Mance, the month is June and the year 1936 – I am four years old. Mother and I are visiting mon oncle Emile. This is a dutiful visit, done once a year and always in the summer.

Emile Flümann is Mother's uncle – her mother's brother. Tante Delima, his wife is Mother's father's sister. So this visit fulfills a double duty.

I am grateful to be sitting on the smooth blue brocade sofa – not on the despicable plush one, which, because of the heat and my bare legs can be almost unbearable.

Mon oncle sits in his big chair facing my mother and me. He is the focus of the room – an impressive presence, immobile, mute but dominating nevertheless. Beside him on a small table there is the usual delicate long-stemmed white clay pipe. We speak to him but he rarely answers. When he smiles, there is something awkward about his face and the crinkles move around one eye only. I am curious about the metal strap over one shoe under his trouser leg. In spite of the heat he is always dressed in a wool suit – cuffed trousers, vest, and jacket. There are others in the room but their words have nothing to do with me. I am in my silent world and do not connect with the conversations flowing over me, like warm water.

The door to Cousine May's room is half open, and inside I can see the two large kettle drums. The sight of the glimmering warm copper of these is the delight, the high point of my visit. I lose myself in their golden, fiery glow. It is the only tenderness I feel in the room. My mother who is near me does not radiate tender feelings. I am aware of her fear, which prevents her from being free to express herself. She is afraid of being humiliated, of being judged. She does not have the confidence to be herself. Perhaps she does not yet know her own truth.

A tight silence, oppressive, encloses her. I absorb this but can do nothing. I sense that I would be betraying her if I did not imitate her. What I do is lose myself in the gleaming welcoming warmth of the copper. I'm aware of the presence of the clay pipe – so comforting to see it there on each visit. Finally, my gaze comes slowly round to the clock under glass on the mantle. I am certain that it will never stop its smooth silent comforting motion. Here is something to be relied upon, something that can be trusted, that is free, that is self sufficient, that does not need comforting. It is something complete in itself – nothing is secret or hidden, no emotion. It just moves smoothly back and forth, back and forth.

Jump Off, Nancy King Schofield, 2009

Elizabeth Blanchard

BITCH CURVE

Gerald couldn't quite figure out why he hadn't stopped when he first heard the sound. And the more distance he put between himself and the bend in the road where the incident occurred, the less likely it seemed he would. It might have been the initial delay in recognition, the soft quick thud too discreet and undefined to trigger a reaction. It would have been different had it been the sound of a fractured windshield or the keening of locked wheels across a paved road. Such violent noises would have set off an adrenaline dump, elicited all the appropriate reactions: hands clutching the steering wheel, elbows locked and spine pressing into the soft leather of the seat with one foot on the clutch and the other hammering the brake pedal through the pearl-gray carpet of the Audi. But as it was, Gerald was barreling down the stretch of road that lay between Salmon Point and Bathurst on his way to the hospital, half-listening to the mellow voice of a late night radio host extolling the virtues of a little known Inuit writer, distracted by a thought scurrying on the edge of his mind. What had he hit back where the road curved away from the sea's ledge at Salmon Point?

It wasn't even his weekend to be on call. Gladys had driven down the coast to their summer home midweek. After two patients cancelled their appointments Friday afternoon, Gerald left the office early and made the 45 minute drive out to the cottage. He found his wife sitting on a green Adirondack lawn chair the neighbor's son had dragged down to the beach at Gladys's request. She wore a one-piece white crinkle bathing suit, and a bright orange sarong wrapped around her thick hips. Her freshly-dyed straight black hair gleamed like a crow's pelt in the sun. Gerald disliked the color instantly, thought it too obvious in its attempt, but knew better than to say anything, especially at the beginning of a long weekend. He preferred her natural color, *whatever that is*, he thought wryly, but the thought carried with it an unexpected feeling of emptiness that gave Gerald a sudden urge to clear his throat.

Resting on the large flat armrest of Gladys's chair was a half-filled oversized plastic glass, the kind you find in the seasonal display at Wal-Mart.

"You managed to get out early." She handed him a bottle of beer from the soft-sided cooler slowly folding into itself next to her chair. In it, Gerald spotted traces of her red lipstick crowning the neck of an empty vodka cooler. There was a time that image would have aroused him.

"I see you got the neighbor to cut the grass," Gerald said, eyeing the edge of the lawn where it had been chewed by the blade of a poorly manoeuvred lawnmower.

"Some caretaker. The place was a mess. How much did you agree to pay him this summer?"

Careful not to react to Gladys's aggressive tone, Gerald loosened his tie and slipped off his shoes and socks, yearning to feel the hardness of the stones against the soles of his feet, their sharp edges reassuring. He swallowed a mouthful of beer. "Al Grey asked me to take his calls for him until 8:00 am tomorrow; says he's got some important banquet tonight he can't afford to miss."

Pivoting her chin over her sunburned shoulder, Gladys looked up at him, her dark sunglasses reflecting Gerald's heavy paunch which hung over his belt. Although he couldn't see them, Gerald could feel his wife's eyes pause on him in quiet disapproval.

He instinctively pulled out his shirt so it hung over his pants. "I'm going to change out of these clothes. Need anything at the cottage?"

"Pick up after yourself, we have guests for supper. Nancy just got back from spending two weeks in the Caribbean with her new beau, Todd. I've invited both of them to dinner." Gladys turned her gaze towards the water and took a sip of her drink. "Imagine, going on a trip with someone you've only known for a month." She shook her head and laughed, a hint of envy trailing in her voice. "Nancy tells me he's at least 15 years younger than her."

Gerald, feeling his face flush, turned and headed towards the cottage...

When his beeper went off later that night, Gerald was relieved. As he drove out of the yard, he could still hear them out on the deck finishing off the second bottle of wine of the evening, Todd's voice garishly loud, Nancy and Gladys laughing in high-pitched squeals.

*

The nagging doubt had now mushroomed into a grim anxiety. Gerald pulled the car over to the side of the road. The engine idled as he sat silently with both hands on the wheel. There were no streetlights on this stretch of road. It couldn't have been a bird, not this late, not in the dark, unless it was a bat. And it had to be at least the height of the door to make that sound or the tires would have simply rolled over it like a speed bump. It wasn't a particularly clear night, but there had been no fog around the point so he would have certainly seen someone had someone been walking. He pictured the familiar bit of road in his mind, how the gravel shoulder narrowed as the road bent sharply around a curve and funneled its way through a thick patch of forest, a sudden crowding of pine and spruce eclipsing any reflections of moonlight the sea might have had to offer. Bitch curve is how the paramedics referred to it, when sitting around the ambulance dock. Young men who had not been on the job long enough or gotten far enough inside the hospital walls to dampen the swagger in their walk. Young men who themselves weren't exempt from joyriding the curve when off-duty on a Saturday night, during one of Salmon Point's infamous bonfire parties.

Why hadn't Gerald stopped when he first heard the sound? His mind was on other things; on the patient whom the nursing supervisor described as stable but needing attention. And yes, the radio was on, he might have been fiddling with the stations, had his head down, or he might have been distracted by the music. But he had definitely heard something. Eyeing his cellular on the dash, the thought of calling the police crossed his mind. He imagined two RCMP officers squatting near a dead dog, poking its blood-matted fur with a stick, making some wry comments in their Quebecois accents. And there was the matter of the wine. He cupped his hand to his mouth and exhaled. The question would be asked. Annoyed with his own indecisiveness, he began pulling away from the roadside when he first heard it: the screech of a siren weaving its way in the night towards him. He became very still, his skin barely able to contain the pounding of his heart as he sat and watched the flashing red lights come into view then disappear from his rear view mirror. He wondered if Gladys and Nancy could hear the siren from the cottage.

Gladys met Nancy when Gladys decided a cottage was needed to fill the wasteland that had become her life, or at least that's how she explained it to Gerald after he'd returned from the hospital late one night. She said it in a calm voice, lying in bed as Gerald took his pants off in the dark. The next day Gladys contacted a realty agent, Nancy Atkinson, a small divorcee with a voracious appetite for new things.

"Gladys tells me you're an orthopedic surgeon," was how Nancy introduced herself the first time she met Gerald during one of Gladys's many parties. She lowered herself onto the arm of Gerald's living room sofa, Perrier water in hand. A silver anklet bracelet dangling from her thin ankle bone, her raspberry pink bra-straps clearly in view under her sleeveless blouse, Nancy held Gerald's gaze and smiled at him as though he were a potential buyer. Gerald, unaccustomed to such male-like boldness in a woman, felt an instant discomfort, the kind of discomfort that arises when stumbling upon the illicit. In retrospect, Gerald would like to think that it was Nancy that pursued him. After all, wasn't it Nancy that came over to their cottage that weekend looking for Gladys when she knew Gladys was on a shopping trip with her sister? Wasn't it Nancy who offered to cook supper for him, who stayed too late discussing property values?

"I get the impression you'd sell anything," Gerald said, allowing himself to slip into Nancy's promiscuousness, his fingers feathering the back of her neck.

"And do anything for a sale," she replied, the intent in her voice, Gerald thought, unmistakable.

In hindsight, that's where Gerald could have stopped it, gone no further, a momentary arousal dealt with later in the privacy of his bed, alone, with Gladys in mind. But it didn't happen that way, and after the initial release, with Nancy's thighs still straddling his hips on the living room floor and her hands pressing his against her small sagging breast under her unclipped bra, he could feel the guilt thickening the air in the room.

"That was my daughter Rachel," Nancy said evenly as she flipped the cellular phone shut. "She needs the car early tomorrow morning." She smiled thinly while pulling on the straps of her high heel shoes. "Smart girl, that one, she knows her mother's bad habits so she's not taking any chances."

Gerald remembered Rachel from the party, a pale sullen 18 year-old in a frayed jean jacket and thick black eye-liner who kept fingering the three tiny studs in her nose when she wasn't checking her cellular to see if she had missed any calls. "How did she know you were here?" Gerald's voice cracked, suddenly jarred by the magnitude of his transgression.

Nancy stood in front of the hall mirror, a hairclip clenched between her teeth. "Relax Gerald," she said in a brassy tone, both hands twisting her copper colored hair in an unkempt pile on her head. "She called on my cell-phone. And besides, she's pretty discreet." She softened her smile and touched his face. "Hmmm, you were wonderful, hope we can do this again."

Never again, thought Gerald, grappling with the sudden weight of infidelity, not as much his own as what he foresaw as Nancy's lack of discretion with her daughter. This he perceived as inevitable as if Rachel had been standing outside with her face cupped to the living room window.

But boredom has its own way of undermining resolve, and as Nancy had hoped, they did do it again, mostly in Gerald's office after hours. Nancy would simply show up on occasion after the secretary had gone home and sit in the waiting room reading "Ask Your Doctor" pamphlets until the last patient left. At lunchtime one day, anticipating one of Nancy's visits, Gerald bought her a jade pendant. Its oval shape and smooth contour appealed to Gerald. He showed it to Nancy that evening as she took off her sunglasses and unfastened her blouse. An hour or so later, Nancy picked the pendant off of Gerald's desk and put it in her purse on the way out. That was the last time she came to his office.

*

Gerald slowed the car to a crawl taking no notice of the police officer waving him past the scene of the accident. His eyes were riveted on the body being lifted unto a collapsible gurney wheeled to the side of the road and illuminated by the headlights of two police cars, their neon green and red strobes lending a surreal eeriness to the scene. In the odd angle in which the right leg lay, Gerald recognized a twisted deformity of the pelvic bone, probably fractured, the right leg no longer in proper alignment as though the head of the femur had been wrenched from its protective socket. He imagined the surrounding ligaments stretched beyond functionality, the smooth neck of the femur snapped, exposing its trabecular marrow. He had seen such bones, touched them, guided wires into their centers through tiny drill holes, inserting pins and fastening screws, always confident in his crisp ability to restore full rotation, or have the final say in those beyond repair. But what lie in wait for him tonight could not so easily be fixed or passed on to a colleague. He sat clutching the wheel, unable to take his eyes from the sight

A car honked loudly behind him and for the second time that night, he pulled over to the side of the road.

It suddenly occurred to him they would be looking for the driver of the car that hit the man. He jerked the door open and stepped out into the sound of voices and car engines made sharp by the cold night air. He made his way around the front of his own car and walked slowly towards the back along the passenger side, running his hand along the door and the angle of the trunk looking for any telltale signs, the metal trim cold under his sweaty palm. The fibers in his lungs tightened at the thought of the contorted body being wheeled towards the ambulance. Was his lawyer's home number in his Blackberry?

"Dr. Owens?"

Gerald hadn't heard the young paramedic come up behind him. Short and stocky, the young man looked like he had just walked out of a weight training session, his white short-sleeve shirt tight around his neck, arms and chest. "Afraid you're too late on this one, Doc," the paramedic said expanding his chest with self-importance. "It looks like he fractured his pelvis and crushed his rib cage on impact," he continued, spreading his feet apart and crossing his arms. "We suspect he probably died of internal injuries."

Gerald felt his stomach heave.

"Too bad. Just a young guy, a kid really. The police tell us they broke up a party at Salmon Beach earlier, figure the teenager must have decided to walk home."

Gerald wished the young man would just shut up.

"And check out the guy that hit him, not much older than the victim."

Gerald's head spun as though he had just been struck. He looked at the paramedic who was nodding in the direction of a police cruiser. In the dark, Gerald could make out the silhouette of a man leaning against the police car, shouting while gesturing vigorously to two officers standing in front of him in their glossy blue-black jackets and bulbous-toed boots. The man's movements were exaggerated and uncoordinated.

"That's the driver of the car that hit the poor bastard," said the paramedic as he slipped his thumbs in his belt and shook his head disapprovingly. " He's high as a kite. His girlfriend was in the car with him when the accident happened," he pointed to the back seat of the cruiser.

For the first time since stepping out of the car Gerald took in the surrounding scene. Just beyond the ambulance, on the opposite side of the road, an old Dodge Charger had rolled half way into the ditch, the front bumper scarcely visible at road level, its back wheels barely touching the pavement. An RCMP officer, with what appeared to be a surveyor's measuring tape, squatted in the middle of the road where black tire marks darkened the pavement while another held the end of the tape and walked slowly the length of the skid marks unwinding the tape, its metal edges glinting sporadically in the police car headlights.

Gerald felt the muscles in his legs weaken. He leaned back against his car, bending at the waist and bracing his hands against his knees, desperate to keep the blood flowing to his brain.

The relief was overwhelming. He hadn't killed a man after all.

"Are you ok, Dr. Owens? The paramedic had lowered himself unto his haunches and placed his hand on Gerald's shoulder.

Gerald stood up abruptly and walked away from the car, his relief beginning to give way to feelings of foolishness. The man in police custody was increasingly belligerent, shouting incoherently while trying to pull himself away from the officers restraining him. Keeping his distance, Gerald circled the police car and found himself standing on the passenger side when he saw the girl sitting in the back seat. The door was open and as Gerald's eyes grew accustomed to the dark, he recognized the girl.

Rachel looked small in the back seat of the police car. Her dark hair, stringy and matted, hung over a bandage covering the width of her forehead, the right side of her temple bruised and beginning to swell. She looked up at him. He struggled with his thoughts, wished he had never gotten out of the car, all the while feeling obligated to say something now that she had seen him.

"Are you ok?"

Rachel said nothing, raised her hand to her face, her index and thumb nervously fingering the studs in her nose. Gerald was about to offer to call Gladys at the cottage, knowing full well that Nancy would still be there drinking wine, when he noticed the smooth oval hanging around Rachel's neck. He recognized the jade pendant he had given to Nancy. The sight of it made Gerald face flush with heat, recalling images of Nancy riding his lap in one of his examining rooms at the office, his pants down around his ankles, her greedy insistence, his own eagerness pathetic. He turned to leave when Rachel finally spoke.

"You won't tell my mother, will you?" Her voice was quiet but defiant. She did not look up at him.

How ironic that Rachel should be asking him not to betray her.

"You know I can't do that." He said evenly, trying to conceal the spite in his tone, "you know that regardless of what I do, she'll eventually find out."

Rachel was quiet for a moment, as if weighing the veracity of Gerald's comment.

"He's right you know," she continued after a few minutes.

"Who's right?" He turned towards her, growing impatient with the situation.

"Nick, my boyfriend," she tilted her head towards the young suspect now face down against the hood of the car, being handcuffed by the officers who were quickly loosing patience. "It wasn't his fault."

Gerald's beeper went off. "I have to go."

"It wasn't Nick's fault," Rachel raised her voice.

Gerald stopped, wanting the conversation to end, the smell of exhaust fumes nauseating.

"I'm expected at the hospital," he said.

"The guy was already down, he was already lying in the road," Rachel was now looking directly at Gerald, "Nick turned hard to avoid him and we ended up in the ditch," she paused and held Gerald's gaze. "It wasn't his fault."

Gerald felt a tightening in his chest and throat, his hands fell to his side like weights on a string gone limp.

"They'll eventually figure it out," Rachel's voice dropped as thought talking to herself, "figure out that it wasn't Nick's fault."

Gerald looked over at the boy pressed up against the car, then beyond the boy, down the road beyond Bitch curve, where the taillights of the ambulance disappeared into the dark patch of forest, its siren noticeably silent.

MOULDED TROPHY-MEN

Linda's been waiting for Tony to come home from working the late shift at the mill; she listens to him undress in the dark.

"Robbie's coming down with something," Linda says. She's been in bed for over an hour. "He was awfully tired after school today." She hears the clink of Tony's belt buckle and the loose change in his pockets. "It's Saturday tomorrow, why don't you let him sleep in."

"He'll be fine," Tony says dropping into bed and turning his back to her, pulling the sheets over his shoulder.

"It's not a tournament," Linda insists. "I'm sure they can do without him just this once."

Tony doesn't answer.

"For godsake Tony. One game, that's all."

"Christ Linda, I just got home from a 12 hour shift. Do we have to do this now?"

Linda stares up at the ceiling, one arm draped across her forehead. The fold of skin on her upper arm feels fleshy and fat, reminds her of how loosely it moves whenever she towels herself stepping out of the shower. Before long, Tony rolls onto his back. His eyes are closed and his mouth open; when he breathes, something soft and pendulous flaps at the back of his throat. All she has to do to stop the snoring is give him a push. Shut up, she thinks.

"Shut up, Tony," she says just loud enough for him to turn on his side, but not so loud as to wake her son Robbie in the next room.
The room is dark except for the dim halo of streetlight extending beyond the sewn edges of the curtains. Linda's eyes are drawn to the dark lump in the chair at the end of the bed, a pile of clean laundry. Tony's shirts hang off the back of the chair. She no longer irons them. She decided not to anymore when pulling clothes out of the dryer one Saturday morning. Tony had just left for the arena with Robbie and the house seemed particularly quiet.

How smooth the ceiling looks in the dark, she thinks, even the nail-pops all but disappear at night. She turns in bed and looks at the back of Tony's head, at his heavy shoulders, at the small fold of fat at the top of his spine. It's his silences she no longer can stand, dense and bristly, like having to lie against a hair shirt.

At first she thought it might have been the room. She painted the walls in pastel colours, hung bright cotton drapes over the window and even spent six months worth of her savings on a down comforter the color of vanilla ice cream.

But this silence of his, it seeps into things, stiffens the fabric. There

89

are nights when she feels her own skin tightening under the sheets. Linda shifts her hips to the edge of the mattress. Unable to settle, she slides out of bed and leaves the room.

The floor feels cold against her bare feet. Her thighs and hips jiggle loosely under her nightgown. Running her fingers along the wall waist high, she makes her way in the dark toward Robbie's room.

When Robbie was younger, Linda used to lift his blankets and slip into bed next to him, wrap her arm around his small frame cupping the underside of his chest in her hand, and fall asleep with his pulse secure against her palm.

But Tony said that Robbie was too old for that. "Boys your age shouldn't be sleeping with their mothers." He said it one morning standing in Robbie's doorway, his back straight and his feet apart.

Linda, helping the boy make his bed, caught how Robbie's cheeks flushed.

That was two years ago. Robbie was six.

Now, on sleepless nights, she sits quietly in the chair next to her son's bed, traces in her mind the curves of his changing face, smoothes the ends of his dark hair against the flannel pillowcase with the back of her hand. There are no sharp angles in this room.

It's in these quiet moments Linda likes to imagine that her mother might have done the same, visited her room while Linda slept, knelt by her bed mouthing soft words in the dark. But that's not the way it was. As a girl, Linda slept on a pullout in the living room and her mother, Bertha, rarely whispered. And although Bertha appeared to relish the words she used on her only child, they were never soft.

"When are you gonna get that damn hair of yours cut?" Bertha leans over the bathroom sink peeling a long dark hair off the bar of soap. She's wearing gray nylon stockings and an unbuttoned red polyester blouse. The bathroom is just off the kitchen. The apartment is so small that everything is just off the kitchen. From the table, Linda can see her mother's pitted thighs and the roll of skin bulging from under her heavy bra.

Linda puts her spoon down and pushes the bowl of dry Frosted Flakes away from her. "We're out of milk."

"It's because of the boys, isn't it?" Her mother's voice fades as she disappears behind the bathroom door to grab her skirt hanging off the hook. "You think they like it long, don't you?"

Linda gives a sharp tug on the hem of her light blue sweater, smoothes it over her flat belly thinking she'll never let herself get fat.

"I work until nine. I don't want you out late." Bertha says sharply, fastening her blouse.

"There's a game tonight."

"You're asking for trouble, girl, hanging around that goddamn rink all the time."

Linda slips on her jacket and lifts her hair up and out over her collar.

"People talk you know." Bertha continues in a low voice, as though talking to herself. "Christ, I can just hear them now. Bertha's girl is boy crazy, gonna get what's coming to her."

Linda zips up her boots wishing her mother would just shut up.

"You best watch yourself. If you get pregnant, you're on your own."

Holding her schoolbooks tight against her chest, Linda walks over to the bathroom purposely scuffing her heels against the linoleum. She glares at her mother. "I'm not that stupid."

Bertha's face turns red; her jaw tightens.

Regret suddenly swells in Linda's throat. She turns and hurries out of the apartment. Her mother follows her to the door in her stocking feet.

"You'd better be home when I get back from work tonight, that's all I got to say," she yells after her with a husky voice. "And next week, you're getting your hair cut, girl!"

Linda never did cut her hair in high school; in fact she made a point of not tying it up. It hung down her back, long and defiant. She didn't care if the boys liked it; what mattered was that Tony liked it. Linda never missed any of Tony's games; she always sat in the stands just behind his bench. She would watch the way Tony leaned in on his skates shifting his body between and around other players never quite stopping or starting as though all his movements were part of one uninterrupted rush. Maybe she believed that he could move through her like that, touch her with his magic, make her life fast and supple like him.

And those nights after the games, her shoulders up against a wall in some dark corner of the arena, Tony leaning in close, whispering something nice in her ear, what she meant to him, the way his finger touched the hollow at the base of her throat as though she were stitched in velvet.

It wasn't what people thought.

Linda hears a car drive by, its headlights briefly illuminating the silver- and copper-edged trophies lining the windowsill in Robbie's room. Above Robbie's bed, Tony's old hockey jersey hangs on the wall, number 18. Robbie says the jersey brings him luck. "It makes me a winner," he tells his mother. Tony was wearing it the night Linda went into labour. She was staying with Tony's parents. She woke her mother-in-law, Fleurette, and asked if she would drive her to the hospital. Fleurette sat in the waiting room until a nurse informed her she had a grandson.

"What a handsome boy," Fleurette says approvingly, sitting in the chair next to the window, holding her black leather purse in her lap, her coat neatly folded over the back of the chair.

Linda is embarrassed by the wet stains on the front of her night-gown and by the odor of her own skin. Seeing Fleurette bend her head and gently pat the stiff curls on the nape of her neck, she wonders if the smell carries over to where her mother-in-law is sitting.

"How are you feeling?" Fleurette says in a concerned voice.

Linda turns in bed and the stitches between her legs pull at a tender spot. Her breast and abdomen are sore, filled with a heaviness not her own.

Linda watches the older woman stand, smooth the wrinkles off the front of her skirt, and walk over to the bassinet at the end of the bed. Fleurette's pearl earrings and butterfly broach seem so delicate, refined. Still holding her purse in both hands, the older woman leans over the baby and smiles sweetly. "He has Tony's eyes and mouth, don't you think."

"Did Tony say what time he was leaving Rimouski?" Linda asks.

"He's on his way. Have you decided on a name?"

Linda arms and legs feel sticky. "I'll wait for Tony."

Fleurette straightens her back and pulls her purse up under her breast, "I'm sure he won't be long." She moves back to the chair and picks her coat up. "I should let you rest. Is there anything I can get you before I go?"

Later, after the nurse had washed Linda, unwrapped the newborn, and gently placed him in bed next to his mother, Linda watched the baby's eyes grow heavy as he sucked on a bottle of milk, milk that didn't smell like milk but something much sweeter. When the baby fell asleep in Linda's arms without fussing, as though her body were a soft, warm place to be, Linda rang the nurse and told her she had decided on the baby's name: Robert James.

Her son's name is the only thing left that carries a trace of her in this room. Robbie believes that Tony's hockey jersey 'makes him a winner" because Tony's team won the night Robbie was born. Linda notices she is often absent in the retelling of the story of her son's birth, just as there is nothing of her in those small molded trophy-men in helmets on the window's ledge, knees bent hard and hockey sticks in hand, their skates frozen in full stride. Novice, Peewee, Atom, most valuable player, this is Tony's language.

Linda pushes herself off the chair and places her hand on Robbie's forehead, checks an impulse to tuck herself in beside him, remembers what it felt like to hold him close. Her feet are like ice when she steps into the hall. Reluctantly, she crawls back into her own bed, avoids any part of her body touching Tony. In the quiet of the room Linda can hear the electrical hum of an appliance, a faint background noise towhich nobody really listens.

NOT OF THE BUCK FORD TRIBE

It's 8:35 a.m. and I'm waiting for the phone to ring. I've been waiting for the call since Monday. They told me they would call me back before the weekend; let me know if they wanted me to come in for an interview with the Program Director. Tomorrow is Saturday and if I don't hear from them soon, the tendons in my neck are going to snap from my vertebrae in a popping sound.

I'm standing at the window of my basement apartment. My view of Regent Street and the tenant parking spaces are obstructed by a snow drift, wind-whipped and crusted, the base of which is butting up against my window, blotting out much needed daylight, darkening my already dingy mood. I should just get off my ass and go out and shovel it. But the problem is that I don't own a shovel. My father does, but my parents' house is a four hour drive from Fredericton, an inconvenient fact for someone who doesn't have a car.

I guess I could always borrow a shovel.

Connors, the building manager on the third floor has one. I've seen him on occasion carry it in and out of the pre-fab utility shed at the back of the parking lot, but oddly enough I've never really seen him use it. I thought of buying a shovel the last time Buck gave me a ride to Regent mall.

The phone rings and my heart bucks like a bull.

Racing across the room, I pick up the receiver. I mouth hello into the phone but my voice sounds embarrassingly weak, mucus sticking to my vocal chords like pine sap. I promptly clear my throat.

"Hello,"

"Is Buck there?"

My heart clunks down into the pit of my stomach.

"Buck." I place my hand over the receiver, ignoring the person on the other end, unable to suppress my disappointment which has instantaneously taken the form of irritation.

"Buck. Phone. Make it quick, I'm waiting for an important call."

Silence

"Buck!"

The bedroom door opens and Buck and all his bulk meanders out like a bear out of hibernation, the elastic waistband of his boxers buried deep beneath the huge mass that is his stomach, an appendage which Buck is incessantly rubbing in an absentminded kind of way, as though responding to some deep seated need to polish the surface into a perfect sphere. His short blond curls lay flat against his temples, making his face look even squarer, his nose and cheeks seemingly broader than usual, as if someone inserted a small straw under his skin while he slept and blew a bit more air into his jowls. His piercing blue eyes and distractingly thick eyelashes, which Buck calls his lady-killers, seem like a freak of nature this morning.

"Who is it?" Buck says, rubbing his left eye and his bulging abdomen simultaneously.

How should I know?" I hold up the phone, my arm fully extended when handing him the receiver.

"Oh-ho, aren't we bitchy this morning?" A slow grin spreads across Buck's face as he bends one knee and lays both hands on his hips in an exaggerated feminine gesture.

"Just take the phone, Buck."

"Chill Bill, why so nasty?" Buck puts both hands on his belly, his smile definitely locked into mocking mode.

Not in the mood for Buck's teasing, I raise the receiver to my mouth. "He'll call you back later."

Before I can hang up, Buck lunges at me, yanks the cordless phone from my hand and plunges onto the futon, which moans miserably under his weight.

"Yo. Big Buck Ford at your service," he says into the phone, winking at me.

"Don't tie up the phone, Buck. I'm serious, man. I really can't afford to miss this call."

Buck, already laughing into the phone, isn't listening. He rolls onto his back, slips his free hand behind his head, and bends his knees so that his kneecaps are now just barely surpassing his belly button riding high atop his massive abdomen.

I hover over him menacingly, resisting the futility of the moment until something in me gives and I walk back to the window brooding, wishing I had a shovel to clear the fucking snow out of the only goddamn window in this apartment after which I'd use it to pummel Buck in the forehead.

The incessant tapping of a keyboard behind the cubicle partition nearest where I'm sitting is making me jumpy. Occasionally, the tapping stops and gives way to the thrum of office chair casters trundling across carpet in a push-and-roll kind of rhythm. The partitions are lined up in Orwellian fashion the length and width of the warehouse-size space, the occasional head popping up randomly from a cubicle only to disappear again in this ergonomically-correct maze. The aluminum nameplate on the office door through which I will soon be asked to step with skills and resume in hand, reads Helen Gallant, Program Director in black block letters.

Nervousness is whirring like a propeller in the hollow of my stomach. I slip my index finger behind the knot of the tie I borrowed from Buck, and tug at it in an attempt loosen the noose. I feel like a fake in my suit, at risk of being fingered at any moment and carried out of the building by two large men in dark suits, my heels dragging across the carpet. I discreetly finger the tiny scar on my nostril where my nose ring used to be, a remnant of my free-thinking past, a philosophy I have quietly put aside since I have become increasingly aware that nothing much is free. I smooth the scar, worried that it will be recognized during the interview, pointed out as an innate and irreversible character flaw as does my grandfather every time I go home for a visit.

My maternal grandfather lives with my parents in the northern part of the province. A small pulp and paper mill town along the Restigouche River, a river, according to my grandfather, teeming with Salmon in the days when thick-chest men rode the spring melt down the Restigouche on logs.

"*Des saumons aussi long qu'ma jambe, Zacharie,*" my grandfather boasts, as if the size of the fish caught had something to do with the strength of a man's character, some bygone measure of virility, which can leave you feeling emasculated if you can't afford a canoe or don't live near a river in which to fish.

"Salmon as long as my leg, jump right in the goddam canoe."

"Was that before or after the mill added the third sulphur treatment pond, pépère?

My grandfather's tales of the days of *les vrais hommes* when fish were more abundant and men were cut from a supposedly sturdier cloth, drive me to distraction, fuelling my feelings of inadequacy, which seem to be growing exponentially since my most recent foray into the job market.

A grey haired man leaning over a partition is talking to someone unseen in the adjoining cubicle. He leans forward and snickers, his voice dropping to a whisper. He's wearing a red sweater vest over his white shirt and his bald spot is quite visible from where I'm sitting. The scent of popcorn drifts across the vast office space and a phone rings. I imagine someone licking their fingers before picking up the receiver. I've been waiting in this chair for over a half an hour, the shirt beneath my armpits now damp. The waiting is winding my string so tight, it's about to pop. I stand and stretch my legs.

Quite unexpectedly, a tall, emaciated man in a wrinkled brown suit emerges from the Director's office next to me. His head is down. The door of the office closes shut behind him. He looks up, sees me. His jaw is so taut it looks wired.

I smile expectantly.

"What?" He says, the word sounding more like a dog's bark then a question.

Uncomfortable, my eyes settle on his noticeably large Adam's apple.

"I'm here for the interview." I say rounding my eyes and smiling foolishly.

"Oh." He says in a more distracted tone of voice. He hugs his file folder to his chest and walks away.

Feeling awkward, I walk over to the windows that line the entire wall between the corner offices. Three floors below me, a constant flow of people move up and down the wide steps of the building, their shoulders and the hems of their winter coats bouncing slightly as they carry their bodies up the concrete steps, heavy accountant cases in hand, bulging with what I imagine are sophisticated documents containing complex information I most likely will be expected to know. I wipe my palms on my pant legs and inhale deeply in hope that the air might contain some elemental substance that will bolster my courage which is beginning to sag miserably.

"Mr. Cormier, please, have a seat." Helen Gallant a tall, pale woman with dark hair set in a heavy bob, points to the seat in front of her desk. Her crisp white blouse looks almost luminescent from underneath her black suit jacket, and, as far as I can see, she has no breast to speak of. She comes out from behind her desk to greet me, a scent of disinfectant soap wafting off her skin. The femininity of her high cheek bones and long neck is soon neutralized by her firm handshake, wide stride and sensible-heeled shoes.

"Sorry to have kept you waiting, Zacharie," she pronounces my name in French with the stress on the second syllable. "We had to deal with a bit of a crisis here this morning." There is subtle but definite hint of annoyance vibrating through that last sentence. I think of the man in the brown suit and feel a what-are-you-getting-yourself-into kind of queasiness in the pit of my stomach.

"Matthew Pike, our recruitment officer, will be helping me out with the interview this morning." She points to a heavy set man sitting of the corner of the room. His white shirt is thin, so thin as to be unintentionally revealing. He raises his head from his clipboard, smiles perfunctorily and nods, but says nothing.

"Would you like some coffee or water before we start?" Ms Gallant has already returned to her seat behind the desk and gives no indication that she is even considering fetching a glass of water for me or anyone else.

"I'm fine, thanks."

"Let me begin by telling you what we're all about, Zacharie. Student Financial Services is responsible for delivering government sponsored financial assistance programs to citizens enrolled in post-secondary institutions." She straightens her back and rests both elbows on the desk, her palms pressed together as if meticulously reciting a prayer. "We are a branch of the Employment and Learner Financial Assistance Division and we answer to the Minister of the Department of Post-Secondary Education, Training and Labour ..."

I bend forward and listen hard, intent on grasping key words in order to insert them into my answers later, concentrate on my body language, endeavour to make eye contact at every opportunity, put into play all the *how to* tips listed on the countless job interview websites I've scanned and on which my mind lingers. I lose focus. I no longer hear what she is saying. Not wanting to appear confused and in an effort to find my bearings, I lower my head for just a moment and, to my dismay, I see that in my nervousness I've inadvertently rolled the copy of my carefully crafted resume I brought with me into a tight little tube that could just as easily be lit up and smoked. Panicking inside, I raise my head and oblige a calm and attentive expression while surreptitiously surveying her desk for another copy of my resume, praying that she won't ask me to supply her with one. Neither do I wish to unroll the one I have in my hand, for fear she will in fact recognize my resume and that the sight of it will incite her to ask me to hand it over, after which I picture myself unrolling it on the desktop and smoothing the curled edges with my elbows. The sound of Buck's horse laugh is ringing in my head right about now.

Buck thinks I'm a fool. He told as much the day I finally got the call inviting me to the interview. He told me while still in his boxers, saddled up to a kitchen chair, ignoring the intermittent beep beep of the microwave behind him.

"Don't do it man," he said; his huge belly is flattened against the back of the wooden chair, his flesh filling in the spaces between the spindles, an indelible image of anatomy gone awry.

"Working for the government is something you do when you're forty, Zach. It's a major dead end.

"This apartment is a major dead end."

"Come out to Alberta with me, there's still time" he persisted, assuming a dogged expression like he was determined to rescue me from the clutches of conformity. Usually, I'm fond of this side of Buck's personality, his platoon-sergeant devotion to his buddies, ready to lug your wounded body off the battle field under enemy fire. But his Buck-knows-best attitude was beginning to deflate my balloon which had me floating on the ceiling the moment I received the call from Ms Gallant.

Beep-beep.

I pointed to the microwave. "Your mac n' cheese is ready, Buck"

Buck pulled the chair out from under him with surprising agility. As he opened the door to the microwave, the sharp smell of powdered cheddar filled the apartment.

"I know a guy who can get you on with me at the CNRL's construction site north of Fort McMurray," he said while shovelling a spoonful of orange pasta into his mouth. "We can live right in the company dorms. It wouldn't cost us squat."

Buck is the kind of guy that doesn't really see the point in spending another year completing his business degree when big money can be made swinging a hammer or wielding a blowtorch, skills Buck comes by genetically, his father being a mechanic and jack of all trades. I, on the other hand, under my schoolteacher-parents' tutelage, was taught that education was an end in itself, ergo the degree in philosophy. And, at home, when it came to fixing things, well, we simply called on my grandfather, until he fell and broke his hip, then George Doucet, a long time buddy of my grandfather, was the man to call. The truth of the matter is I'm not of the George Doucet or Buck Ford tribe, that clan of men, like my grandfather, whom you turn to when in a fix and who confidently shrug off what they cannot fix as irreparable. The truth of the matter is, a truth I'm not particularly inclined to share with Buck, is that I would be totally useless on a construction site north of Fort McMurray, Alberta or anywhere else.

I'm suddenly aware of an expectant silence hanging over me.

Helen Gallant has stopped talking and is looking at me like it's my turn to say something. Even Matthew Pike has raised his head from his clipboard and is no longer scribbling.

She must have asked a question. I didn't hear the question.

"Pardon me?" I venture, my heart thumping wildly.

She pauses, then smiles forcibly.

"I was just saying that you should tell us a bit about yourself, Zacharie." There is very little warmth in her tone.

I desperately try to remember the notes I jotted down in the margins of my resume which now looks like a long thin reefer, but I'm drawing a blank. It suddenly occurs to me regardless how I answer this question, it's going to sound artificial, come off as a fabrication? A car horn honks loudly in the street. I hear a suppressed sigh emanating from Mr.Pike.

"What would you like to know?" I say politely.

Clearing her throat, Helen Gallant pulls a file folder from the corner pile of papers on her desk, rolls her seat in even closer to the desk and speaks at a faster pace, moving on to the next question.

I have a sinking feeling that I am not doing well here.

"Do you have any experience in customer service?"

I think back to the summer from hell spent in a small office with six other students wired to a headset taking verbal abuse from irate voices complaining about damaged or lost goods.

"Yes, I worked as a customer service representative for a parcel shipping company for the summer."

"Can you give me an example of a difficult situation you encountered and how you handled it?"

The question is unexpected; every call was a bitch. "It's hard to remember specific calls. "We processed so many in a day."

"What about difficulties with management or colleagues at work."

"I had a manager who wasn't very accessible." The middle aged freak locked himself in his office and surfed porn sites for hours.

"And how did you manage that?"

I avoided the jerk didn't seem a fitting answer at this point in the interview. I look over at Mr. Pike who has once again lowered his head and has begun writing on his clipboard.

"If I had any problem calls, I was directed to pass them on to a senior staff."

The door opens, the emaciated man in the brown suit leans through the opening in the doorway. From where I am sitting, I can only see him from the waist up. He silently motions with his bony index finger for Pike to follow him out into the bullpen.

Pike begins to push himself out of his seat, then appears to change his mind midstream, looking over at his boss who is now glaring at the man in the brown suit, her eyebrows frighteningly arched.

"Yes, John?" she says.

"I need Matt."

"Can't this wait?"

Pike's ass is still only half off the seat, not certain what to do.

Skinny Johnny retreats into the doorway to the point where only his head, adams apple and left shoulder are visible. Using the door as a shield, he utters in a squeaky voice. "You're the one who told me it had to be resolved this morning."

There is a pregnant pause as his comment hangs in the air for a moment with no place to land. I imagine seeing a puff of smoke roll out of Ms Gallant's nostrils as she rises from behind her desk.

"Excuse us, Zacharie."

Skinny Johnny disappears; Ms Gallant exits the office with Matthew Pike in tow.

I am left alone in the office. I quickly unroll my resume on the desk and smooth out the corners with my fist.

I hear the door open behind me, Pike leans in.

"Ms. Gallant wanted to thank you for coming in. She has to deal with an urgent matter right now. We'll give you a call if we need more information. Can you find your way out?"

I stand and turn to answer but Matthew Pike has already disappeared, in his place a small women in a blue pantsuit walks by with stack of photocopy paper. I pick my curled resume off the desk; the notes in the margins are in my handwriting: *the study of philosophy teaches students to assess problems from different perspectives enabling them to better recognize alternative courses of action when dealing with an issue.*

I look at my watch; 3:45 p.m. Buck must be flying over Winnipeg right about now.

THE GODLINESS OF THE BLACKSMITH

> *Our pictures of the body's parts will especially sat-*
> *isfy those who do not always have the opportu-*
> *nity to dissect a human body, or if they do, have a*
> *nature so delicate and unsuitable in a doctor that*
> *though they are obviously captivated by a knowl-*
> *edge of humankind that is most pleasant to them*
> *and attests the wisdom (if anything does) of the in-*
> *finite Creator of things, they cannot bring them-*
> *selves actually to attend an occasional dissection.*

Andreas Vesalius, *De Humani Corporis Fabrica*,
1542 (Thoughts on the visual Arts and Anatomy)

Vesalius takes pleasure in the smell of the corpse, they said, the hand of Lucifer at work. But I could not believe this. I paid little attention to such simple-mindedness. It was not the cadaver that excited him, but the strange glistening fabrics that he found under its skin, straps of dense flesh so carefully folded into each other that one could not tell at first sight where and how they were fastened to the bone. I can still hear the rustling of his black robe as he paced behind me, his beard scraping my ear as he leaned over my shoulder and thrusts his fingers down on my drawing. "The lines, here and here, why are they not symmetrical?" I felt his hand clasp my shoulder as he pointed to the carcass at the center of the room. "See how the muscles of the torso unfold perfectly to either side like the inverted wings of a moth. You must see, see with the eyes of an artist."

He was right.

Where most looked with fear upon the lolling head of a corpse, he appeared to revel in what lie under the pleats of skin he so skillfully pared from the chest, neck, arms, and legs. He insisted time and time again that I touch the braid of thick fibers that stretched over the shoulder, instructed me to push my finger between the taught ropes of muscle and witness the hardness of the bone for myself. Only then, he lectured me with his intelligent eyes, would I know how to trace the texture of the muscle to his liking.

We met in Venice, at the Master's studio. Over time, he convinced me that no one else would do. I suspect that it is only because the other students were suspicious of his endeavors. Like mice, they scurried around me on the steps of the school in the evening upon my return, whispered to me in the rising shadows of the pillars of his unholy ways. His work is blasphemous, they hissed, their lips curled as though relishing the sound of their own gossip lapping against the damp stone walls of the city, the smell of mold in their nostrils. They counseled me against consorting with such an immoral figure. Did he not rob the innocents of their bones in the cemeteries of Paris? Did he not steal a body from a gibbet in Louvain. As they spoke, my eyes were drawn to their soft necks and jowls and I was tempted to bring my hand up and find the sharp angular line of the jaw bone buried beneath.

I must always draw the body upright, Vesalius insisted, noble and with the dignity deserving of the ancients and the men of medicine who will study these drawings. To do this, I had to position myself near the table. A complete view of the subject required that I stand and look down over the corpse, which lay with its palms and chest heavenward, the head lodged between two small fingers of wood secured to the table. My earliest sketches were unsuccessful, being as yet unaccustomed to the foul stench of three-day-old carrion. But Vesalius was patient with my first faint-hearted attempts, my nights made restless with the thoughts of these lost souls. The public dissections were the most trying, my view often hindered by the many distinguished men of the guild attending the dissection, physicians, surgeons, and the curious odd wealthy merchant crowding in around the table. It was important that I attend, Vesalius believed, for the most perfect bodies were saved for these occasions. This was before the clerics of Spain denounced Vesalius for dissecting a body in which the heart still beat, before his practices were increasingly vilified, and forcibly, of a more clandestine nature.

It was in this agitated state of mind that I was ordered to accompany him to a public hanging in the piazetta on the Feast of all Saints. Standing at the far edge of the gathering, the hood of his cloak pulled low over his eyes, Vesalius looked on with notable contempt at the scene. Men, women, and children pushing in on each other to better see the condemned on the platform of the gallows. I felt ill as the olive-skin prisoner dropped through the opening in the planks. I could not prevent my heart from pounding nor the tightening in my loins as the mob cheered when the body jerked. The ill-fated man struggled violently, if only briefly, against the weight of his own mass, his legs kicking wildly at the empty space under his feet, as though beating back the bloodlust of the crowd. His hands bound behind his back, the muscles in his arms glistened with sweat in the cold sun. Watching the body sway long after it stopped flailing, I felt light-headed.

Before leaving, Vesalius discreetly dropped a few coins into the palms of two ragged-looking men who did not seem entirely unfamiliar to him.

Draw him as he was in life, Vesalius urged me, the remains of the olive-skin Venetian lying on the table before me, the underlying fabric of his shoulder, neck and head already exposed. Without the thick beard, black hair, and pox-marked skin, the face on the table took on a peculiar gracefulness. Broad, fine lines stretched across the jaw, sultry shadows pooling in the hollow of the cheeks and eyes, the missing ears adding an unusual smoothness to the skull. Suddenly taken by such strange beauty, I began to draw the man as I wished him, Herculean and defiant. I traced the lines vibrant and strong, sculpted the cheek in tones of ash, outlined the long thick filaments of the throat free from its noose. I moved closer to the table, sketched the hardness of the flat bone at the center of the chest, carefully reproduced the strength and symmetry of the abdomen and thighs. As I continued to draw feverishly, I became exhilarated by the realization that there was no truth in the vulgar belief that dissection prolonged the agony of the executed beyond death. There was no suffering in what I saw before me, only exquisite form.

It is at this very moment of clarity that Vesalius leaned in close and inspected my work. "A simple blacksmith," he said, the words spoken softly, his foul breath against my cheek, "accused of thievery, poor fool."

Untitled 2, Roméo Savoie, 2009

Lee D. Thompson

MOVING HOUSE

A man awakes to find his house is underwater. He wakes to shadows on a wall, to a darkness that allows shadows. Shadows that move like shadows. Shadows moving like a film, or a like dream. Shadows wavering.

He lifts from the floor, and he says this to himself, says someone has done it, someone has moved my house underwater, says it with certainty.

He moves through the hallway, which is dark with shadows. He moves slowly through the hallway seeing the shadows, the floor, wavering like something he remembers, can picture but not imagine. A night or a dream.

At the end of the hallway there's the salon. He stops at the end of the hallway, uneasy. The salon is sunken, circular, and the windows are long like walls. There is furniture, a table in one corner, and two chairs. The table is round. There is a rug, and it too is round.

Is this my house? he says. Someone has slipped it through something, I feel I know how, or why, know that this is possible, to slip a house through something, but why I know escapes me the moment I reach for it.

The salon is sunken in shadows, and a darkness.

The man has entered the salon, feels the weight of the ocean. It's not possible, but it has happened. When things slip through, he says to himself, you have to accept it, or else you go crazy.

In the salon, he has a sense of things. After all, he is safe, no one would build a house that wouldn't stand up to this. The man sits at the table and runs his hands over the marble surface.

There's a silence in the salon, a breathing silence, he knows he's not alone. There's the sense of things slipping, of a clock that breathes, strange things. He looks at his hands. He looks at the windows, sees a distant light, faint, fading. Sees a jagged crack in the window, a trickle.

After all, no house was built for this.

He stands, knows he shouldn't be here, that none of this belongs here. The sense of time is the thing, the thing that's under him, that's slipping, sudden vertigo far below the surface. He leans against a window.

It's a strange, strange light, he says. It's an exhausted light, a light that's lived too long, end-of-the-universe light.

The man wanders along the windows, sees more cracks. He wanders along, wonders why they wanted so much light. Why did we think it was such a good thing?

He pauses, seems to recognize or recall something.

Yet all of my life I've had a sense of this, that one morning I'd awake to this, and here I am. In a way, it's comforting. Except that I'm frightened. Because when the house was chosen no one thought of this, no one asked: is it well-suited for the Depths? How well-sealed are the electrical outlets? The windows? The letter box?

The man wanders along the windows until he reaches a door. The door is slightly open, should open to the sea, but doesn't open to the sea. It opens to a room. A light is on.

He pushes the door, sees a woman. She's sitting at a table.

What have you done to the house? he asks her.

The man enters the room, sees that it's a kitchen, the shelves are bare, a basin gleams. She's sitting motionless, but breathing, she's nervous. She knows she's done something, has broken something. Slipped something through? Yes, she knows. She moves her head a little, says hello? Is someone talking to me?

There are cracks in the windows, he says. What have you done to the house?

It happened while he was in bed, yes, she had done it. Yes she had done what she had said she would do. Had warned him, had said I'll do it, sorry but one day it will happen, and there's nothing you can do about it. And here he was. The sense of slipping was, he knew, no sense at all. The sense of time slipping was something else.

The cracks in the windows, he says, they shouldn't be there.

She shakes her head, again says hello?

None of this is right, he says.

She sighs.

Does she know him? He asks and she laughs, almost embarrassed, says of course I do, you're in some mood, you.

He moves to take the chair next to her. He tells her it's not safe here, that there are lots of problems, I don't know where to start. He's sitting next to a tall shelf. The shelf, empty, is made of glass. The glass contains bubbles. Next to the shelf is a calendar, dates are circled, and below the calendar is a curled photograph.

He stands and looks at the photograph: it's faded, shows a man in a glass box, hands tied behind his back. The box contains water, and the man has drowned.

Who is this man, he demands. Why is his picture on the wall?

It's attached, she says.

I don't like it, he says.

He tears the photo from the wall, then leaves. He's returning to the salon. No, he's returning to the bedroom. He moans, feels he can't take another step.

He sits at the marble table, regards the rug at his feet.

From the kitchen he hears crying.

The salon's rug is red or brown, hard to tell in the light there is. There's a pattern on the rug, but he can't see it. He's looking. And when he does see it, he can't understand it. There's a circular pattern of fish swallowing what could be rabbits. The could-be rabbits' eyes are black and wide with fear.

No, he says, I never bought this rug.

He lifts it from the floor, holds it in front of him.

One would say these fish are primordial, not yet sure what a fish is. They are spiny, everything about them is spiny, and they were made for swallowing. But are they land stranded, or have the rabbits fallen into the sea? Or am I looking at this the wrong way, and are the fish giving birth to rabbits? Or is this one creature?

The man sets the rug on the floor. For the first time he feels the sense of slipping is real. It's not a sense. The ocean is sloped, he thinks, sloped and always falling. No, the house wasn't built for this, no house was built for this. No house has been put on skis to go sliding through the sea-bottom.

Stop crying, he calls.

He hears a door shut.

She wants to be alone, whoever she is.

But yes, it was she, she who had done it.

Oh he knows she has her ways, that what she says she'll do she'll do, she'll find a way. Certainly she took steps beforehand. And I had no idea, he says, though I knew too well.

My house is underwater, he says. The air is cool and dark, and I feel alone, and I feel as if a mouth has opened, has taken a deep breath and all there is to do is scream. But the mouth can't scream.

In the salon, standing with both hands against a window.

The man wonders if others are having the same problems, sudden house-underwater problems. He wonders if there are others at their windows, distressed. There must be someone to call, someone who knows. Because the windows can't keep it up, can't hold it back for long. He sits at the marble table, head in hands, until he hears singing.

It was often like that, he whispers. Night, the windows open, a summery wind.

Hello? she says. Heading across the salon, walking briskly. Hello? I don't think the shelves will stock themselves. Idiot. She's holding a raincoat and she's descending stairs. I'll be back when I'm back, she calls.

She comes back up the stairs, stands at the top of the stairs, says why have you turned off the lights? It's not like you to like the dark.

The man at the table lifts his head. Do you realize what will happen if you open the door? he asks.

I asked you a question, she says.

It is not made for this, he responds.

She goes down the stairs, he hears a door open, hears a door shut.

His hands play over the table's marble surface, then the salon is in darkness. Something passes with powerful strokes, the house rumbles, creaks, the cracks in the windows multiply with a sound, disconcerting. He feels vaguely ill. The house has slipped, he says.

He stands, searches the windows, sees distant lights, little else. Why she had done it, he'll never know, though he does. He moans, says I know too well. After years of telling me.

She's floating off somewhere, he whispers.

The man thinks of the rug, the nightmare fish. Thinks maybe it's not a rug at all, but something from the letter box, and that makes sense, he says to himself. After all, I was sleeping, so I am out of the loop. Yes, everything has a reason.

And what if the rug truly is something from the letter box, something like a welcome but be careful, if you see this, danger, danger, don't swim nude out of doors sign?

He moves across the salon, to an edge where the stairs fall darkly. At the bottom of the stairs he finds a door. He gropes for the door handle, finds it, opens the door, finds another room, dimly lit.

She's standing before a window, staring out. The room is small, semicircular. He asks her what she's waiting for. A taxi, she responds.

A taxi.

Called one hours ago.

How long will you wait?

Not much longer, she says.

Listen, don't go out there.

It's really raining, yes.

Please, he says.

She turns to him, smiles sadly, says she's sorry things haven't turned out so well. I've been moody. It's just...

She slips off her raincoat, is in his arms, her kisses are warm on his neck, his chin, her hands seeking. Quickly his hands slip to the underside of her thighs, he lifts her. He takes her while the shadows waver over their bodies. His orgasm is forgettable.

While they lay still the man's sense that the house is slipping is strong. There's the sense that they will be tumbling freely, that an abyss awaits everything. An abyss where nothing lives but the strangest of fish, he thinks, fish with too many eyes, and where nothing dead ever rots. Our house will be there for millennia, canted, murmuring, gathering the pale bones of whales...

Her hand on his thigh, she says, I dreamed this morning that there was grain in the letter box, golden seed, all compacted, as if it had been there for years... I tried to dig it out... because the letters were being taking by the breeze...

He leaves her, returns to the salon.

He has the feeling there's something that must be done, a word spoken, a gesture made, that something has been forgotten, as if one were seeing a clock upside-down, confused, unable to tell time because the clock's stopped breathing, that's what it is, the air, the air. Where is our air coming from?

Was there soughing and now there's not-soughing? He quickly searches the walls, slides his hands along surfaces, hands encountering nothing but shadow, and when the walls end there are windows, and they're more cracked than ever.

The man feels he has to take action, feels he has gone too long without taking action. In the centre of the salon, hands in his hair, he seeks solutions. Something has to be done to counter what has been done.

He regards the rug.

Footsteps and she crosses the salon, doesn't speak to him, raincoat over her head.

He lifts the rug, holds it before him.

I don't like it, he says. The kind of rug that gets under your skin, stays there till your flesh is interwoven with it. He shakes it vigorously. Not exactly a welcome mat, is it?

Is she crying again?

Unravel the rug, the man thinks. Unravel the rug and use the unravellings to clog the cracks, that would work. But first consider the cracks, the amount of rug, and other things. Calculations. However, this rug must have a purpose. She's left it here for me to see.

The man closes his eyes, sets the rug on the floor.

Yes, he hears crying.

But it's better she's crying in the bedroom than heading out for groceries.

The house rumbles anew, this time the walls shudder, a picture frame falls to the floor, the marble table tilts, the chairs slide, the man finds himself reaching because he's falling, reaches for the marble table, the chairs, falls. The salon is black now, so is he blind?

I've fallen so hard I've forgotten how to see.

The house continues to slide. Soon the salon is lighted a deep blue, and dark again. Lights flicker by, grow fainter. Then more lights, more deep blue. And dark. But it's not the lights, he realizes, it's the house, the house. It's not moving light, but moving house.

The house has sped past a small village.

Again, he's ill. Perhaps, in her haste, she forgot to secure the foundation? And now a current of ocean wind has taken them, has no intention of leaving them. He tries to get to his feet, but his head is spinning. He moans.

He turns over and vomits on the rug.

When his head has stopped spinning, he realizes his plan for repairing the windows won't work. He's never seen a window repaired with rug before, it's not a stroke of genius. And even if he washes it thoroughly... which he must do. The trash can was always left outside the front door, he recalls, would find it on its side in the morning. Where is it now and why such sentiment?

He thinks it's important to think straight.

He must talk to her.

But she won't be happy with the rug, certainly it's hers, for he never bought it and doesn't like it. She might accuse him of vomiting on purpose, as if he'd vomit on anything that displeased him, like something pulled out of the sea, sickened by the sight of dry things. She's in the bedroom. She's wailing, or is it sobbing?

The man folds the rug, brings it to the kitchen. In the kitchen the photograph has been replaced with a child-like sketch of the same, in blue and red. Little arrows point to the drowned-man's eyes.

He sets the rug in the basin. The vomit clogs the drain, so he reaches for the tap. But what will happen when he opens the tap? He takes a deep breath, is stunned by the stench, feels the panic return. He imagines a supersonic spray, the rug torn to shreds, the basin dented.

And if my hand had been below?

He leaves the rug.

He removes the sketch from the wall and tears it in half. He hopes she likes that, this woman always singing always sketching, sketching things like curtains and boxes, bridges and windows. Jars. Other things that smash when it's to time go. I'm not impressed, he calls out. With everything you've done, you think I'm supposed to be impressed? Well I'm not!

Yes, that's all she wants, he says to himself. Look at me, that's all she wants. Poor me, yes. Sad me, yes.

Feeling reckless, he returns to the basin and opens the hot water. There's a trickle, brown, tepid.

The man washes the rug. If we stay here, he thinks while washing vigorously, we'll be taken the by the deep ocean currents. An image comes to mind, of something with a shell, something shifting along the sea-bottom. They say so much of the seafloor is unmapped, we'd be explorers, and so we'd have to name our house. But what about food? Could we cast a net out a window, catch strange things and, smiling, eat them? She could sketch all that she sees, the dark seaweed mountains, the fields of beady-eyed fish, the purple, clam-enshrouded gorges...

The house shudders.

But of course the windows won't hold up.

The house shudders, the man catches his balance. I've been under the spell of this damn rug, he says. And why am I cleaning it when I detest it?

She's still crying.

In the salon, he casts the rug aside, fish and rabbits spinning in the shadows. The windows show something soft and luminous, the light plays in the cracks, unlikely lightning.

There was an old city, he whispers, an old city in ruins. We were there for the music, then a storm came. We wandered the narrow streets, drenched in it, in search of a temple, Zeus, the storm rumbling in the stark hills...

She liked the rain, but I was soaked through.

From the hallway, her sobbing. She won't stop and he knows it, knows this will go on and on. And with all that she's done? The man would prefer not to listen to her, but where can he go? What a hell she's created, he says, then shouts, what a hell you've created!

He finds himself before the bedroom door.

Open up and stop crying, he says.

Go away, she says.

He leaves, but once in the salon he returns.

This is hell, you know. So open up.

What do you know about it? she asks.

Years and years, he says, that's what I know about it.

Go away, don't come back, you can't come in.

Why not?

I can't do it anymore.

And the rug?

I can't do it anymore...

Let me in, please...

I can't pretend anymore...

We have to talk.

It's too late, she says.

The man knows it's too late, that there she is, everything is too late. Leaving the door unlocked when he left was no help, but what could he do? He had wanted to help, but what could he do?

I vomited on it, he says. I did it on purpose.

Sobbing...

Let me in?

The man hears bedsprings, shuffling of feet. No, she says, her voice at the door. I need to be alone, she says. Do you think you could go out for a while, let me be? I'm sorry, but I need to be alone. Think of it this way, you need to be alone too. So it's a good thing. Okay? Hello? Things will be so much better like that, right?

No...

I really need to be alone.

No... listen...

If you love me.

At the door, head against the door, the man thinks he'll get in the car, drive... find the rivers, the bridges, the winding roads, drive...

My house is underwater, he says.

Is that it? she asks.

Listen...

You want me again, she says.

No... listen...

I'll open if you take me, she says.

The man, hands on the door, sobbing...

Take me, swing your hips against mine, but don't say a word...

Please...

Swing your hips, your sex in me, feel my legs wrap around you, feel my mouth on yours... promise me?

The man is sitting on the floor.

If you do that, I will let you in, but not for long.

Something calls him to the salon, he's on his feet though he still hears her, though he doesn't understand her. And she's tall, he says, with long black hair, so I don't know her, don't know anyone like that. I don't know anyone who cries like that. Who would say such things to me.

The solution, the man thinks, would be to get rid of her. A little less hell, he thinks. Push her out the door, perhaps. Or batter her with the rug.

In the salon, he searches. He's not sure what he's looking for, there's water on the floor, he knows he's seeking something, he hears it.

The telephone.

In a house racing along the ocean floor, the telephone is ringing. This can only be ominous, this the man knows, senses that answering the telephone will shatter something, and maybe it's the windows. That the telephone is ringing disturbs me, he says, and I should plug my ears.

He searches but doesn't find the telephone. He searches the wall, can't quite place where the sound is coming from, again feels with his hands, puts his ear to the wall. He enters the kitchen, says why don't they just hang up? Back in the salon, the ringing continues.

He closes his eyes, moves a few steps. Yes, the ringing is coming from there.... he opens his eyes to see he's standing on the rug.

But it's not the rug that's ringing, he says. Will you pick up the rug, it's your mother. No one ever says that.

Mother, how nice of you to have rug me up.

The telephone, he sees, for another village is racing by, the salon is lighted, and everything beyond, which is other houses, streetlights, all dim yet there, is lighted, and the telephone, he sees, is on a wall jutting from the house, a white wall out there.

Oh, he says.

It stops ringing.

There never was a way to answer it, he says. Wasted so much time searching for it. Strange to think that any stranger could have picked it up. That any old person could know all of your business, have a laugh at your expense.

I have to get out, he says. But that's not an option, he says. I could move to the kitchen, or I could move to the room where we made love, or I could cry some more at the bedroom door. There are options but I don't much like any of them. This whole situation unnerves me and I can't seem to relax. I would just like to lay a while on the bed, forget things, close my eyes and maybe hold her, or strangle her, I'm quite confused about things.

She did it, she did it all. That she had this in her he's never doubted. The man is moving toward the hallway to the bedroom. She's difficult to talk to, he says, and she frightens me.

Screams now, from the bedroom. Perhaps objects being thrown.

And the house, shuddering, a rapid vibration. The man's heart stops when he sees what he sees, for the house is racing through a chasm, walls of grey rock inches from the windows. He's transfixed, never realized just how fast the house was moving.

Where are we headed? he whispers.

Oh what strangeness, the man thinks. Caught in the middle like this, between her screams and these walls. I've always hated you, she screams. Whoever you are I've always hated you. You annoy me.

The man, paralysed in the salon. With the vibrations things begin to fall, the windows crack further. The marble table, the chairs, seem to move of their own will. This, the man thinks, is surely the end. And it's what I deserve for having slept and dreamed, while she lay in a corner of the bed, curled in agony, making her plans.

Yet in the morning she'd lay out over me, her eyes narrowed and voice purring, her sex slick against mine, rubbing.

The man sits again, somehow the house is holding up. Maybe it was built for this, built to bend but not to break, built to get the heart pounding. Maybe there are others, houses in front of us, houses behind us, and it's all wild screaming and sex. A party. He doesn't believe it.

Beneath him fish and rabbits, nightmare teeth. The table is on its side, there are cracks in the centre, and cracks in the floor, cracks every-where he looks. Stay here and watch it all? Hide somewhere? End it all with one flung chair? And the things he could do in the bedroom, and who would know?

The man's head is in his hands.

Stop, he pleads, please stop.

And then the worst of it, the house slamming, shattering. It's hap-pening much too quickly, and he can only close his eyes to it. I won't look, he says. Good God I won't look. We're in the mouth of something, some-thing that's always awaited us. Sleeping and yet it's always awaited us. Every hour of my waking life I've known this.

Shouts, OK, this is what you wanted.

Shouts, OK, OK.

Unsteadily he rises to his feet. One last look at the salon, the light seems to be coming from the cracks, hissing jets of it spray from the win-dows. He stands and the chair falls, the sound deadened by the deafening crashing.

He stumbles at the edge of the salon, enters the hallway, staggers against the wall. The shadows here are crazy, stabbing like daggers.

He's at the bedroom door, there's plaster falling from the ceiling. He's prepared to shoulder his way in but the door is open, hanging un-hinged, the floor distorted. We have to talk, he shouts, though she can't hear him. He says it one more time, because he has to know.

A lifting jolt and he's on the bed, face down, the bed sliding to the wall. Once against the wall he notices the wallpaper, and it's the same as the bedspread, it's strange fish swallowing what could be rabbits. There's not much light but he sees it, he knows what it means. My God, he says again.

Then he turns over.

There's perfect silence.

Hello? she says. She's nude, standing half in shadow. I'm sorry about the mess, she says, I just can't keep up. I slept so terribly last night, dreamt of grain, and now nothing seems to fit. Everything I put on, it falls off me. Hello? What should I wear this evening? I can't decide. Help me decide. Maybe we should just stay in, do you think that would be better? We could rearrange the closet, empty it out, then sleep soundly. We could do that. Hello? Can you see me? Can you see me now?

Why are things so silent? he says.

Quiet, she says.

The house is falling, he says. That's it. It's falling like a leaf in the air, or like a stone in a sea. I awoke this morning, and I found this, the shadows on the wall, the wavering shadows and then the salon, all that water. And not aquarium bright, but dark, like night.

But this far down it always makes night.

He lifts from the bed and moves through the hallway. In the salon he stumbles over the table, the chairs, stops at the jagged window. Below, but approaching, he sees the dark awaiting, the nightmare teeth. From the bedroom she is calling his name. He falls forward and floats toward the shining surface.

THE LOLA TOOTH STORY

It was early morning and Lola was making our breakfast. She was wearing her white kimono, the one with the red flowers, her brown hair was tied back, and I was smiling, sitting, waiting, and then Lola's tiny hand started to tremble. She was pouring our coffee and then she slammed down the coffee pot and our coffee, in great dark blooms, flew all over her kimono, and the table, and the toast. Well, when she had rolled out of bed that morning, with that short sigh of hers, that hint of a growl, I thought I had sensed a little tension.

When she looked at me, I stopped smiling. I made a big pout, reached out my hairy arms and wanted to say come here my darling and I will make everything better. But Lola spoke first, my beloved Lola, and when Lola told me just how much I disgusted her, her voice coming from some deep and troubled place, my tooth fell out. Well, it's hard to stand tall, feeling your left upper canine sitting on the tip of your tongue, tasting your blood. And unfortunately there's nothing that incenses Lola more than slouching. She let me have it, again and again. Stand straight and look me in the eye, she said. Be a man for once!
I guess this had been building up for some time.

But Lola, I tried to explain, my tooth has fallen out! My eyes were wide with astonishment, surely she'd come running to me saying my God, what have I done? I'm not in a good mood this morning, let's go into the bedroom and make love. But Lola didn't do that. Lola's tirade continued. Lola, in her ruined kimono, the one I bought in Sapporo during our first anniversary, she started to throw our breakfast dishes to the floor, she was trembling from head to foot, and her little fists were making sharp, sudden gestures.

I rushed to the washroom. Yes, I knew she thought I was fleeing, a coward, that I had turned my back on her but believe me, that wasn't the case, my tooth had fallen out! Lola, come look, come look in the bathroom mirror, come see what you've done. Come see what an awful morning this has become for me. Before the mirror I opened my mouth and the tooth, a huge purple thing, fell into my hand. I looked to Lola. My sweetheart was leaning in the doorjamb, her arms were crossed and she was sneering. And when I opened the palm of my hand and showed her the tooth she stormed off.

Yaya, I called.

Well, amazing thing, this tooth. It was at least three times as long as I suspected a tooth should be. The root was a dark violet and deeply curved and grooved. It glistened in the washroom's glare. From the kitchen I could hear pots and pans and I thought maybe Lola was calming herself by doing the dishes, which was good of her, seeing that they had been piling up for a couple of days now.

I took a deep breath, held the tooth by its tip, and made the first attempt at reinsertion. But my hand was trembling so greatly that I nearly inserted the tooth into my nose! The pain in my gums was ferocious and I was sick to my stomach imagining the shocking pain of insertion. On my second attempt I squeezed the tip of the tooth too tightly – it was slick – and the tooth flew, arced high and clacked off the edge of the toilet seat and dropped onto the shaggy mat. Well, I scrambled after it, stayed on my knees, then closed my eyes and placed the root of the tooth at wound's tender opening. I breathed deeply, quickly...

And jammed it in there.

Surely Lola could hear my howling, surely she'd come to my side, hold me, kiss my forehead, make a sad face and caress my hair? Surely she wouldn't leave me like this? Lola, Lola.

But no Lola.

I staggered to my feet, rested my elbows on the wide, spotless lavabo, then steadied myself. Yes, Lola, I will now come out and talk to you, I will have an open mind and I will listen whatever silly bee is buzzing under your bonnet. I will coo when you tell that me you did not sleep well, or that you just haven't felt yourself of late. I will smile and tilt my head when you tell me that you feel shackled, that love is nothing but a shabby rat's trap. So I opened my mouth, readied to take a deep breath, and then my damn tooth fell out again! It hadn't caught. I would have to hold it in place but the slightest pressure caused my knees to stagger. And then I gagged.

Miserable morning.

Yaya, I called, wanting to ask her if our dentist, Doctor Pittio, had returned from her vacation.

Bur Lola didn't come. Walking to the kitchen I thought perhaps she's left, but she hadn't left. She was sitting in the sun, at the breakfast table, leaning back, arms still crossed. All around her was the destroyed kitchen. Lola, I know you are not happy, but now's not the time. I held my hand to my mouth, tried to speak these words, tried to explain the cost of dental surgery, the agony of the cutting and stitching, all the blood, tried to chastise just a little, for she had been very careless, but then I stopped myself, because of the look on Lola's face.

When I sat across from Lola, Lola stood.

And oh, the look in Lola's eyes, the fury when I suggested she change out of her kimono. But I honestly thought she'd feel better if she did. It wasn't my intention to further incense her. But the moment I said kimono she threw off the kimono and then tried to tear it. Yaya, I said, perhaps it's not ruined yet, perhaps we can clean it. Don't you cherish this souvenir of our days in Japan? Lola paced the kitchen. Lola turned, pointed at me, shook and screamed. She wouldn't stop screaming and stomping her feet. And then she said it again, said that she was so sick of me, how every moment of her life with me was torture, and how the thought of spending another minute with me made her want to find the nearest dagger and jab it into her heart. And then she found a jam-smeared knife on the floor and picked it up. Was this the Lola I knew and loved, who would hold my hand and caress my forehead when I'd get a migraine?

Yaya, let's talk about this. You are not being very rational this morning. What have I done that's so awful? What you are saying, Yaya, is very hurtful. Listen, Yaya, we'll drive to the hospital together, and maybe later you can have a session with Doctor Marcosi? Wouldn't you like that?

But her fist was white around the handle of the knife, and she pressed the tip against her left breast. Yaya, I whispered. Her eyes were closed and she was crying. Yaya...

Dazed, holding a hand to my mouth, I wandered into the bedroom, looked at the unmade bed, gathered a few things in a suitcase. When I returned to the kitchen my beloved Lola was still there, nude in the morning sun, eyes closed and the knife to her heart. I think there was a trickle of blood. I didn't dare kiss her goodbye.

And so I found myself on the street, my head low, famished for breakfast, some toast and steaming coffee. A sparkling sun was rising over the city but my heart was torn and I didn't much care about the sparkling sun. I knew I needed to see a dentist, and I knew I needed to find a hotel room, and I thought: But how easy all of that is, when it only takes a phone call.

So for an hour or two I lingered around our apartment building, sitting in the lobby, me and my suitcase, and when our neighbours would pass I would smile sadly behind my hand. Tell her, I would say, and they would regard me curiously. Later I went outside and sat on a bench, a bench that was a few floors below the kitchen window of our apartment. And often I put my head in my hands and wept, my shoulders shaking, knowing Lola could see me. Well, why should I hide my misery? At one point I slipped off the bench, and lay at the foot of it, and people came by, asked me how I was doing, offered small change and slipped it in my pocket when I refused. I waited for an hour, but where was Lola's beaming smile?

Yaya, Yaya, I whispered.

When the sun rose to midday I got up and picked the lock to Lola's car, where I slept in the back seat, where I had horrible dreams, and when I woke I opened the glove compartment and, unthinking, ate a chocolate bar. Lola loves her chocolate. There were wrappers all over the back floor of the car, and chocolate stains on the upholstery, and the windows, and Lola often said that nothing, perhaps no one, could ever please her like chocolate could please her. She wouldn't be happy with my thievery. And neither was I. For having just awoken I wasn't entirely sensate, and so I just popped the entire chocolate bar into my mouth, greedily, like a baby bird, and then I realized that I no longer had my tooth! I couldn't find it anywhere. Did I swallow it with the chocolate? Did it fall out while I was sleeping? I searched the floor, under the seats, I searched my clothing, my pockets. I put my finger in the back of my throat and gagged, but other than a few spurts of unsweetened brown chocolate, nothing came up. Would my tooth work a jagged path through my entrails?

Oh Lola, what have I done to deserve this?

And that's what she wants, I told myself. She wants me to come crawling back, to beg her to let me back into her bed. I was supposed to fall to my knees, in the apartment, I was supposed to become hysterical, pull her down on top of me. But instead my damned tooth fell out, and she couldn't have planned that, that was an unexpected thing. I tried to explain it all, but how could she understand me with hand over my mouth and my stumbling tongue? Perhaps she misheard me?

She told me to get out and all I did was mumble in response? Something about a toothache?

Maddening!

Well, I found myself climbing the stairs, and then found myself before our apartment door, the golden eleven. Lola, I've come back. Isn't that a wonderful thing? I straightened my hair, my clothes, checked my breath, tried to hide all traces of chocolate. I heard music, a Greek singer, it was lively music, music that Lola loved to dance and sing to. And I heard Lola singing, and by the stomping I knew she was dancing, so maybe she was no longer mad, so I knocked, and the music stopped. I waited but Lola didn't come to the door, and music started again.

Yaya, let me in. Yaya, let's talk about this. I knocked again, lightly this time, and put my forehead against the door, listened, and for the longest time all I heard was Lola's singing, her voice coming softly, then strongly, then softly. Lola has the most beautiful voice. It's an angel's voice. Many a time had I told my Lola that the world of hairstyling was fine, respectable, but my darling, you have a gift. Her response was not to sneer, but to smile, to stare dreamily at the refrigerator. And then the phone rang and I put my ear to the door. Lola turned the music down, she seemed excited to hear from the caller, she was saying yes, yes, yes, and then she was laughing.

Laughing!

But was this a time for laughter?

Well, I sat at the door and listened to my sweetheart laugh, laugh and make jokes about me, about my belly, about my lovemaking technique, about my love of flowers, about my crying during old movies, about my singing in the shower, about the size of my member, about my snoring, about my love of garlic, and of course my bad breath, about my love of German opera, about my pretentious French, about my mother, my mother, and even about my constant caresses. She said that I was lazy, dull, and an embarrassment, and she wondered why she hadn't had an affair earlier...

She laughed, called herself stupid, then spoke breathlessly of a handsome Romanian.

Miserable, miserable day. I returned to the car. Another late-summer tempest was raging but this was nothing compared to the ache in my gums, which had now spread to the entire left side of my face. In the back seat I remembered what I had dreamed about, and I had dreamed that Lola was standing above me, stomping on my face. She was smiling, had a birthday cake in one hand, a knife in the other.

Evening had arrived but by the heaviness of the clouds it was already night. I rummaged through the glove compartment, found more chocolate, ate it without much remorse. In my suitcase I found an opera CD, Wagner, cradled it closely and then nearly cried when I realized I couldn't play it, that I couldn't start the car, so instead I let the rain, the thunder, be my lullaby, and in the back seat, with my suitcase for a pillow, I fell asleep.

The dream I had is almost too terrible to recount. I found myself in a strange city, a foreigner, I had no home and my body was diseased, my left hand was rotted at the wrist and about to fall from my arm. A procession of military trucks came down a narrow city street and I knew I should hide, but I was too tired to hide, my body was too worn, and then the truck stopped before me and soldiers hustled me into the back of the truck. I was alone. And then the dream shifted to a sort of prison camp, and I was made to wear a ballerina's get-up, the pink shoes, the tutu, all of it, but none of it fit. I would be the embarrassment of the camp, and the ballet had even been my idea! And we were all lepers. I was standing before a mirror in the dressing room and it was to be our first performance, they all were waiting, it was horrible, how would my smile look with my missing teeth, and then the door opened, slammed shut, and I sat up.

The car's motor started and I lay back down.

There was Lola, my beloved Lola, and she was all dolled up. Her

hair was tied back and she was wearing PouPou, which is her favourite perfume, and the car was moving through the rainy streets. Well, I didn't know
what to do. I did nothing. We drove along for a few blocks, Lola was talking
to herself, she seemed nervous, excited, she was sighing a lot, just as she
did when we first met, years ago. She played a CD, which I swear was Romanian, and between that and her perfume and the day's fatigue and pain,
well, I began to weep. But Lola didn't hear my weeping. She drove on until
something started to bother her, she wasn't sitting still in her seat, she kept
fidgeting, I could hear her little exclamations, and then a final, exasperated
gasp. Well, apparently Lola had been sitting on something uncomfortable,
and when she pulled over and held the object of her annoyance close to the
overhead light, we both saw what it was, and it was my tooth. My tooth!
Lola made a sound of disgust and threw my tooth out the window! Did she
realize that it was my tooth? Could she even recall having a husband that
morning?

And then, as if my suffering were not acute enough, she pulled out
her cell phone and called her lover. It's me, she said. Me. Lola. No, I said,
It's me. Yes. Me. Well, she went on like that for some time, I'm in my car,
my car... no, not my church, my car... I'm... in... my... car... Yes, I'll be there
soon... what? No, no... he's gone... gone...

Perhaps, in some other nightmare, one where I have all of my teeth,
I grab Lola's little phone and, in perfect Romanian, I call Lola's lover every
dark orifice of the human body, and associate very unpleasant odours with
these dark orifices, and then I threaten to hurt him, and then I take Lola's
little phone and I crush it in my hand. But in that other nightmare I would
be strong, and not a coward, and Lola would never have left me. The rain
continued to fall, flashes of lightning were seen above the city, and Lola
continued to babble and coo, and then Lola unbuttoned her black blouse,
loosened her black slacks, placed a black-booted foot on the dash...

Yes, yes, tell me more, she was saying.

Well, I slipped away then. From the centre of the street I watched
Lola, anyone could see her, had she no shame? Illuminated, this was my
Lola, whom I had loved like no other. I reached out my hairy arms one last
time, then placed them on my head, then turned around and, suitcase in
hand, walked away.

But everywhere I saw my tooth. Was it fever? Was it stress? What had Lola
done to me? In a dark, filth-ridden alleyway my tooth stood smoking and
looking nervous. I stopped and said hello to my tooth, but my tooth retreated into the shadows. Well, I didn't want you anyway! I shouted and ran. But
where was I running to? I wasn't running to Lola, for Lola was gone. She

had thrown the coffee pot during breakfast, yes, then stabbed her little heart. She had said terrible things to me. At the next street corner there it was again, my tooth, standing under a lamppost. I wasn't sure at first, the rain was heavy, but yes, it was my tooth. I stopped when it seemed to beckon, yes it was leaning forward and gesturing. But I didn't trust it, why was it clinging to that lamppost? What was it hiding? It seemed to have a greenish pallor. Again I ran. But farther down the street my tooth approached me, it was wearing a red silk kimono, and heavy lipstick, it offered me sexual favours for money, and I shouted go away, please go away, leave me alone, why has the world abandoned me, why has this been such an awful day, why has it all turned out like this, why, why, why I ran and shouted.

Then I found myself in a poorly-lit pub.

Well, it was dry there, and the regulars seemed as miserable a lot as I, they were haggard and hollow and yes, they were missing many teeth. I had never seen so many missing teeth in my life! We smiled in mutual sympathy, and I felt I was home. Soon the drinking began, and though I've never been much of a beer drinker, having always preferred red wine, something with a bouquet of plums or raspberries, well I drank till my liver cried for mercy, drank till my liver cried and then stopped crying, for it had been drowned. I sang songs with the toothless, I arm wrestled the bravest, I hugged and kissed the boozy, gap-smiled women, I told them about my Lola and then we drank to my Lola, and it was all good fun for a while.

But soon I started to cry, and I couldn't stop crying. Oh, Lola, oh Yaya, oh Lola, I wept. And then I called my friends all the names I had wanted to call Lola's lover, I called them horrid examples of humanity, I called them heartless mutants, I called them the dreg-noughts of society, and I told them they made me ill. My friends stopped buying my drinks. I told them I had seen who they truly were, and they weren't kindred spirits at all, they were vile and weak. And in protest I vomited on the bar. Well, after that they turned on me, they began to pummel me, they loomed over me, kicking me, swinging their hard fists.

But I had the last laugh.

From the floor I flashed them my picture of Lola, and they went silent. They discussed it amongst themselves and then helped me to my feet. One of them even brought me to the hospital.

And that's where I am today, Lola. My beloved Lola. I am feeling so much better now. The doctors say oh, a tooth, that's nothing, we can replace a thousand teeth! And I ask them, But will it be the same tooth? And they promise me it will look exactly the same.

And that's the best I can do, Lola. I'm here, waiting, my Love. I've even had the nurse set aside a spot for your flowers, when they arrive. But

please, please wait till I've been stitched up, then you'll see, then you'll see:
my broken smile, good as new.

Feral Goat, Nancy King Schofield, 2009

Nancy King Schofield

It might be easier
to fail with land in sight
than gain my blue peninsula
to perish of delight.
                    - Emily Dickinson

The Opening

It wasn't unlike being in life
navigating these estuary rooms
hearing the silence of oars slide through
light and reflected moon.
Voices heard in the distance meted
insult on snow white day lilies,
left them slashed, dripping scarlet
in the corner while we looked away.

Long lines of faces stared in disbelief
at his tale of stormy seas,
that pulled his boat until it fell away.
How arms of crystal kept him warm
with hair of grass until the shore was reached
and tongues dripped honey
in his pale cold ears.

Before wandering away, wouldn't you
agree that being loved isn't easy on a
daily basis, could be dangerous
when it's all mixed up?

One time in Italy his sea legs roamed
the bare peninsula, blue like his heart when
he remembered Emily, felt Emily's isolation.
He saw the house he built for her
felt his fingers digging into rich red soil
to relive a time of little reimbursement.

Eventually he learned how to stay in the boat
and sing out loud in grave yards.

His words like weapons launched
flying missiles. A suitable tool when wielded
works as sure as sphinx moths
but nothing is ever certain.

His blue peninsula was a lifetime
of rooms archived in shadow.
Strips of canvas or paper hanging tattered
haphazard in the end;
a fragile landscape borne of vulnerability.
But to admit that the reachable didn't exist
was to perish in darkness
unable to hold on to the core.
And when we finally get to the end of it
isn't that what art is for?

Life is a horizontal fall.
Opium (1930)
Jean Cocteau

Jump Off

Do men freeze when they yearn to fall out?
Can they be plucked off or sucked back in
like pollen that sticks to the lungs,
before the door slams open-shut?

And what of golden plains seen confiscated
as ravaged gypsies and Palestinians ride
over cliffs onto rocks like the great buffalo,
to be hidden by the millennium?

Will the celestial heat from shooting stars
restore the essence of the critical masses,
or arc angels press down long glass fingers
to poke holes in the canopy of night?

Should rivers of melting icebergs break their fall
as they drop through the starry cosmos?
Straddling glacial fissures, they hover and shiver
along the slippery edge of nothing.

Mongols march in blazing fur hats up ahead
selling lemonade to spectators.
Smiling through betrayal, they spit out words
too dark to be seen with the naked eye.

Once in a cracked mirror I saw a man whose
expression reversed all things planetary.
Herd dogs began to sing and jump on branches,
birds lay on the damp earth and howled.

He watched this master hide while the
servants sipped private Beaujolais from
vintage crystal glasses and fingered heirlooms,
wearing an expression of indifference.
Staring through the open window, they

heard the laughter of children at play.
Watched motionless as they gathered hay
to feed the spreading fire.

Horses tethered at the gate reared up agitated
when smoke borne by the wind tickled flared
nostrils. Wide-eyed with fear, they yanked down
hard on leather leads worn shiny.

Meanwhile back in the parlor, a broody wine
bubbled atonement for past indiscretions.
Anger helped pave the road to now but betrayal
did the weeding, filled cracks each season.

It began by burrowing slowly until the truth
pushed up bloated, like a victim of drowning.
Once discovered, it was reburied in the muck
where it couldn't be seen.

You better stop and listen unless you're madly
in love with loneliness or the color of egg yolk.
All this confusion makes it difficult to hear and
 it is easy to lose the way.

Good advice is to stay home like old folks
as every day is a drama of actors who forget
their lines. Remember to stand on the ledge
with butterflies and believe...you're not alone.

*Jump off!

There is no cure for birth and death
save to enjoy the interval.
– George Santayana (1863-1962)

A Letter to Alex

I remember your hasty arrival
when I saw for the first time
a quivering parcel of fists
that punched at air
and splayed toes kicking hands
that thrust you
unceremoniously
along the horizon line
of my mountain belly.

But the nurse kept twirling
her grey head bobbing
muttering the same words
over and over:
"Much ado about nothing.
 Much ado about nothing."

And so we waited.

I remember clinically crisp sheets that
piled up green like leaves between us
smelled strands of disinfectant that floated
through air and teased nostrils
the clink of surgical steel tossed into
silence by a stressed out doctor
as he took care of business
in the overhead mirror.

But the nurse kept twirling
her grey head bobbing
muttering four words over and over:
"Much ado about nothing.
 Much ado about nothing."

And still we waited.

I remember your eyes open wide
staring back at me for the first time
unblinking,
feeling connected by raw energy
that surged between us
a primordial pull tight as wire
and together we waited
to enter the secret club of genesis
to discover the mystery
of why you chose me.

But the nurse kept twirling
her grey head bobbing
muttering four words
over and over:
"Much ado about nothing.
 Much ado about nothing."

And while I waited,
they took you away.

At the Table

Sometimes on a summer eve
when we weren't disturbed
by some unexpected arrival
we liked to linger at the table
with a good merlot
bathe in the mellow of
Jarrett's jazz
let it gently wrap us
and the room
in long strips of warmth
close like winter wool.

The only interruptions
were sounds of laughter
breaking the silence in
short bursts like an
intermittent fountain
and we felt innate joy
that sharing brings
magic to be savored
when a heart is hung to dry
and the shroud of vulnerability
reappears.

Talk of music would continue
long after the waning sun dropped
saffron strips through a bamboo screen
sliding stealthily across darkened walls
they almost went unnoticed
but for the framed faces
lit by their passing
each image frozen in black and white
from another time in another space.

Words like honey continued to
fill our mouths until
our cheeks bulged
spilling into the sultry air
they flew like moths around

a porch light back and forth
bumping into chairs and lamps
until they crashed down
like stacks of pancakes
and we ate them up.

Feral Goats

The black night in the mirror fell on the road behind us.
Wheels threw up and an image of orphan Annie was
swallowed by a cloud of debris. Her tiny hand
continued to wave until barely visible in the ensuing
dust funnel and it seemed that she had problems with her
eyes or everything was a surprise.

A vintage film in black and white was projected in reverse
on the clouds. We laughed to see migrating elephants slide
off the highway slick with oil, making sounds that were very
Catholic. They say you will forget them before dawn if you
sleep soundly but you can't get too close in dry season.

The decision to take self-portraits with disposable cameras
presented another conundrum. Film crews decided on
chicken, fearing a reoccurrence of bookworm that almost
put them out of business. Divorcees are particularly susceptible
to this malady but understanding their body language often helps.

Plans for the Paris project went a little beyond what one
might call ambitious. Apparently art stops at the retina,
never quite making it to the mind. You can still find people
who love color but in the end it is never enough. One year
I was put in charge of the weather and tended it faithfully.
Spontaneous combustion in the bush became unmanageable
and provided too many mice for adoption. It's fortunate that
fires are just too exciting to be ignored.

When airlines began making cutbacks, it was blamed on
seniors leaving for the crusades. Consuming nuts and pretzels
in economy, surprised those who liked to gather in colonies
and drink orange juice at sunset. I've always thought
conversation at the local watering hole to be highly over- rated,
especially when searching for the perfect meal.

1700 meters above sea level the crew feasted on guacamole
and fish. Their clothes although nicely laundered, displayed
bullet holes from a civil war. Secretly, I took pictures with
my Zenit and spent hours developing negatives in the bathtub

with a retired border official. The sun was so blinding that
I didn't see a fish tipping the faucet as he flew by to take a look.

By mid morning, tourist busses began to arrive that reminded us
of other Peruvian civilizations destroyed by overcrowding.
It's true after all is spread with dung, cheap pleasure rules,
and to both I would say:

"Be ye ever constant. Marvel at the beauty of evolution
and God and rue the day when feral goats will once
again roam the earth, in search of a home."

"You must love the crust of earth on which
you dwell more than the sweet crust of bread
or any cake."
Henry David Thoreau

Frozen Pears

I walked through grey light
under empty skies with eyes shut
trying not to see the day,
or trees stripped bare
of pallid pieces that lay beneath
bleached blanket skies in naked
protest. Their cold branches stretched
to touch the sea that stood still in
empty waves of ignorance.

Banks of nothingness piled all
around me except for the ravens overhead
pear shaped, perched in long lines
that looked strung out and frozen.
Swaying rows reflected iridescent
black of wings tapered in like Scarlet's
lace petticoat but with tail feathers.
.

Sitting immobile, they looked
down and laughed through open beaks
at trees falling on wooden children
and roots that twisted stone ankles.
The wind shrieked at their indifference
as woolen fists slammed down the earth
and cries rose up from bodies
blurred in movement; rhythmic
bending, jumping, twirling.

Paris Suite

One After the Other

Windows we pass by, one after the other
reflect a human parade we must enter.
Following an exterior world mirrored
on interiors, we move along
conveyer belts of space choked with
rhythms and sounds that clang ears
incessantly, unfamiliar.

Others slide by in their transparent
multicolored skin worn thin
through fear or love or loss; fabric woven
from neurons and dangling dendrites.
We watch their eyes and bodies squeeze
together, move away
as if to deny our existence.

Why, if we aren't there?

We swim in this sea of mechanical forms,
each a shrunken power station.
Movement is fuelled by circles of energy
that expand, move out to
fall in pockets and shoes and hair.
Surrounded by layers dripping
fragrant with expectation
we suck it in and wear it like a nor'easter
rubberized for the storm,
armed for the onslaught.

Even French pigeons avoid eye
contact when we pass not noticing
our tendency to hug the curb
(their territory)
while grabbing tiny crumbs
caught in the wake of a pulsing beat.

Stunned by such beauty

138

we scramble across the boulevard
to a café and
sip a glass of wine;
the color of the Moulin Rouge
lined long with legs and lipstick.
Winds blow Paris light
against my face as I follow
your scent like a dragon
recalled from a mythic tale.
And a beggar with stories in his eyes
stands near the subway street
looking down at emptiness
and his dirty feet.

Papa Chapter

Wooden stairs sounded each step of his
labored ascent as he slowly climbed to the
top; sounds that warned of his arrival
and our departure of noisy play.

Thin walls allowed three children to hear
his humming travel up thirteen risers
until he stopped it with his hand
on a highly polished doorknob.

As he stepped into the apartment, I could
hear my mother whisper from the far
end of the kitchen "street angel, house devil"
and she looked down as though unaware,
as if she didn't care.

I watched as she poured thick black
coffee into his cup and carried fresh sliced
bread to his place at the family table.
It always played out the same way.

She never let his mistakes erase the memories
that were good. Working on the railroad to provide
a living for nine was hard for someone
who she said the family never understood.

When he was only thirteen years he ran from
a father who swung a strap with ease; someone
he knew he could never please.
To survive he did the only thing he could

and walked miles of rail each day.
Weeding between ties of wood gave him
five cents each week. I was too young to ask
where he slept at night or ate his food.

One day when she had to be away
he tried to fill my mothers place.
Pots battled plates for space on the table

as we sat down for papa's "yonder dinner."

Three children laughing and playing
missed the sound of dentures clicking faster.
Three kids ignorant of his table rules
had never seen his anger explode.

"Quiet" he shouted and silence fell faster than
his teeth as he dropped them in a water glass.
We watched in disbelief as they floated
to the bottom, smiling distorted pink.

Forty years of coupling railroad cars
left only five fingers on both hands
to count the beads where he sat everyday
in the corner of the parlor.

The old canary waited to sing for him
in a cage overhead and pushed yellow
through the bars leaning close
to his whispered prayers.

Ten Days

Ten days of waiting since a heart dropped
without warning and the sound of glass
cracked through the night like a runaway
train. Light fell in when lives were yanked
from the comfort of childish dreams, thrust
into a different reality; a room full of innocence
and multicolored carpets with fringed edges,
newly stained with guilt and fear.

We were forced to enter a place hidden
beneath skin and bone; a mysterious space
of retracted ribs housing pumping auricular
and ventricular. Lost in red velvet chambers,
we joined the race where heart is king to trump
the knight in a fragile game of chess.

Seven days passed through hazy halls and
shadowed forms moved in and out of your pale
static room. Their anxious mouths made sounds
we didn't recognize like unscripted actors in a
sleazy film; a foreign flick with subtitles and
a miniscule budget. Minutes and hours rang
hollow as empty smiles piled upon your bed.
Paralysis held my clenched hand and squeezed
my lungs until breathing seemed unnecessary.

I watched mute as doctors tugged disinfected
sheets over tubes and trousers. Knowing nothing
but the outline of your body I traced legs and
arms that lay out-stretched with my eyes.
Remembering nothing but metal toy soldiers
lying wounded on a field of battle I watched
you not moving beneath a dark and heavy mantle.

Ten days melted away like Dali's watch and
nurses with metal clinking trays meandered like
tributaries, down long shiny halls. Each day pretty
girls in red rubber boots mopped them clean

while swinging their pails and laughing at things
that clicked and beeped.

> *Death is the last enemy: once we've*
> *got past that I think everything will be all right.*
> — Alice Thomas Ellis (b.1932)

The Burial

When her body came to rest between two paradigms
spray-painted pink doves were released into a vacuum
by the victim of a horrifying mistake. Due to the gravity
of things celestial that are better left unsaid,

many joined the Seven Years' war and soon
died as a result of widespread starvation. Those who caught
bullets seemed to last much longer. A team of noted physicians
became the first combat mission on horseback in nearly ten

decades. Folks hailed them in a ticker-tape parade, wearing
flesh colored flares that filled the air and billowed when they
walked like giant voluminous turkey wattles. Lining the curb,
they reached out to pet plump Palominos in a show of support

but discouraged unwelcome meddling by the naysayers.
Folks who kept their cats in pickling pots and shared
hysterectomies or appendectomies while hanging from the
clothesline; a watering hole for tight- assed locals where

gossip hatched faster than a backyard egg and got served up
just as scrambled. To establish a lead in the race against suspicion
they would have to acquire new skills.
Meanwhile back in the infantry, the physicians began

to speak in tongues. Using this improved form of
communication, they convinced the security forces to
avert the revolution in the Boreal forest. This opened the
area to American developers and a Starbucks outlet made it

impossible for them to leave. Instead they held Friday night
bingo and lived on pork livers and boxes of clean air.
However, the path to personal peace is littered and winding
and few can avoid going wacky in solitary confinement.

Once again, I digress.

When her body came to rest along the shore of the
turbulent Kennebecasis, seven ravens formed a feather
circle that weighed approximately two kilos and oily black
tears thick as depression cascaded between her thighs.

Two Muslims, whose mission was to study lobster dreams
and other mythic tales, lay on starched linen sheets and
watched the ritual in silence. They had been transported
in a jaunty manner across the Dead Sea but now they just

seemed annoyed and threw pop-corn at refugees as they
tiptoed by. Well, in the end we've all got a wall to crash into
so put your head down and go for it dear Annie. See if it gets
you more attention than before.

Before you went into hiding and saw your flame dwindle from
lack of oxygen.
In the end, our only hope for survival rests in door-to-door
delivery of poutine rape. Despite the unusual texture,

the Swiss government declared it effective for the treatment
of hypothermia. Fortunately, it doesn't require refrigeration
when delivered by a St. Bernard.
Skiing anyone…or poutine?

> *Our flesh, Dante, one day*
> *Will be such golden dust*
> *As a storyless wind stirs*
> *In an empty vault.*
> > \- Etruscan Tombs
> > \- Irving Layton

The Picnic

The last time we met it got dark outside, suddenly,
and I couldn't shovel the heaviness until the mood
changed. People dropped in and out according to
the weather but often leaned heavily into the wind,
holding on to trees with their legs.

After lunch was served, chewing continued until
the artichokes yellowed and the pickles forgot to
zing. I remember thinking of nothing more
than five-inch heels until the vet from Virginia choked
on a peanut. This caused a reaction that
exploded to form a cloud and a flock of nuns
blacked out the sun for two days.

After the sandwiches and other wanton bits had been
consumed by the populace, life continued as usual
until the bull was seen strolling leisurely between
tables, like someone recently unemployed. Such an
event might initiate fear and trepidation in some folks
but a strange scientific occurrence caused a pile-up of
red ants that blocked his path. Fortunately for the gathering,
some had evolved beyond the adolescent stage, learning
about capitulation and the art of reading psalms.

"It is easier for a camel to pass through the eye
of a needle than for a rich man to enter
the Kingdom of God." (Matthew 19:24)
spoke the priest to his congregation and a Toronto
camel named Black, slipped through the eye of a crack.

Knowing that people will love you if you're indispensable,
dappled dandelions were gathered and left to ferment until

they effervesced. Skipping girls pink with rouged cheeks
poured gallons into goblets until the mood of the crowd
spilled out into the street.

At least I think it did during a summer solstice
but it doesn't really matter in the end as long as
everyone cleans up and pays the price of admission.
By the way, are you free to gather dandelions with me next year?

Mon guide s'en va, Elaine Amyot, 1990

Noeline Bridge

Visit to a Dying Father

The last time I saw my father he was dying of lung cancer. He had been given six months to a year to live when it was diagnosed the previous December, in 1977. When the surgeon opened him up, the cancer was found to be inoperable. My parents were told that he had about a year left. There was nothing to do but wait and see.

Eighteen months before, on his 60th birthday, Dad had retired from the farm. He and my mother bought a cottage on the estuary at Little Waihi Beach, about 50 miles up the coast of the Bay of Plenty from the farm, and had renovated it and moved there. In her regular letters to me, in Canada, Mum described their new life, now one of leisure, which was richly deserved after years of hard work. Dad had been a youth during the Depression, working on his parents' farm for no wages. Hard on the heels of the Depression came the war, and during it he met and married Mum; she moved into the farmhouse with him, where five of us seven children arrived in quick succession, and where we were all raised. During my childhood, I was aware that he had wanted another career than farming: he often spoke wistfully of owning his own garage and convenience store, like the one down the road from our farm, but money was scarce so he had to remain a farmer.

When I received the news of his cancer in Canada, I had recently been promoted in my library job, and it wasn't until March that I could arrange my work so I could fly to New Zealand to visit my parents. Mum drove to Auckland airport to meet me, along with several family members; she explained that the long car journey would have been too tiring for Dad. We all had lunch at the airport, and a sister-in-law sitting next to me murmured, "You'll see a big change in Dad." I nodded my thanks. Then we dispersed, and after one of my brothers carried my baggage to Mum's car, Mum and I set out on the long drive southeast to the new home. In the car, Mum also warned me that I'd see changes in Dad. I'd been working long hours and the flight from Edmonton to Auckland was very long, so I was tired when we got to Little Waihi Beach. At the top of the hill, Mum pointed out the small settlement around the estuary below, scattered house lights, some reflected in the dark water, and somewhere in the night beyond, the Pacific Ocean. Then we drove down the steep, winding road, and after two short turns, she pulled the car up on grass outside the new house.

An outside light came on and Dad appeared in its glow, looking thinner than I'd remembered. He came out to the car to help with my luggage. He and Mum then led me into a big, lighted kitchen. He had me sit at the table with him while Mum made tea and set out cookies. Not only was the large, modern kitchen markedly different from old farm kitchen, but so was Dad's new appearance from the father I'd previously known, shockingly so, in spite of the warnings I'd received. He had never been tall, but he had been a well-built man with a round face. Now he was thin. His eyes, which had been framed by creases and laughter lines in his plump face, protruded in large, prominent green balls above cheeks that fell flat. His forceful masculine voice had become high and husky. The skin hung slack on his formerly muscled arms. He was so changed I couldn't recognize him as my father, and worse, he strongly resembled a man I knew I had once met. It was as if my mother were now married to that man, and my father gone somewhere else. I kept on looking around at the strange kitchen, and except that my mother was a constant, I would have thought I was with strangers.

"You'll be tired," said Mum, "and Mick usually goes to bed early. So I'll show you to your room." Our farmhouse had been long, with several bedrooms leading off the passage; this house was short, with a small hallway. Mum pointed out the small bathroom on one side and a bedroom with bunk beds – "for visiting children," she said – on the other. At the end were two bedrooms, side by side. "And this is the spare room, your room," said Mum. "Ours is next to it. I'll leave you to unpack and go to bed."

As I unpacked just enough for the night, I heard them talking to each other in the next room, and then the creak of their bed as they got into it – those bedtime sounds were at least familiar to me. When I got into the strange bed and tried to sleep, I was kept awake by a rhythmic booming in the distance. In my disorientation, it took me a while to realize that it was the breakers of the ocean, pounding beyond the estuary, instead of the constant rustling of the wind in the trees lining the drive to our farmhouse.

My eventual sleep was deep and refreshing. When I came out into the kitchen and saw Dad drinking tea and reading a newspaper, looking up to smile and ask me if I'd slept well, and Mum offering me coffee and asking if I'd like bacon and eggs, the disparate elements of the night before assembled themselves into a coherent picture. As they pointed out the features of the kitchen, including the exquisitely fitted mahogany cabinetry made and installed by my cabinetmaker brother, Dad became my father again, just another version of himself, and the kitchen took its place as a proud part of my parents' new home.

After breakfast, Mum drove us to the next town, which was now Te Puke instead of Whakatane, for groceries. When they were together in the car, Dad always used to do the driving. Also different was a detour on the way back, to a health food store to buy apricot kernels for Dad, in a belief that their laetrile could cure cancer; Mum had been a nurse when they married, and both of them had always scoffed at remedies outside mainstream medicine.

After lunch, Mum suggested we drive to the next beach for a walk, to explore rocks and rock pools on the headland dividing the two beaches. Dad would drive the car home, and then have the rest he needed each afternoon. We would then walk home.

Scrambling over rocks and bending down to peer into tide pools to study colourful sea anemones and other small sea life had been part of our childhood holidays by the ocean. But now that had changed too: the pools no longer contained the anemones and other creatures; there was only water. Suddenly I began to cry, bursting out to Mum my impressions of Dad: "He looks so different, in fact like a man I once met. It's as if you'd married him, and Dad was gone!" Our parents were never demonstrative with us, but Mum now put her arm around me. "I can assure you he's still your father," she said. "He's just changed. He hopes you kids will remember him as he used to be, not as he is now." I said, "I know. That's how I will remember him," as I now knew I would.

We rounded the rocky headland to step down onto sand, which stretched a long distance before us. As we had always done on walks along the beach, we walked along the damper, firmer sand near the waves. It was a calm, sunny day, and the ocean was blue and sunlit, the waves breaking gently on the beach. When they first moved to Little Waihi, Mum had bought herself a surf ski, in which she explored the estuary and even ventured out into the ocean. I mentioned this now, and she told me how she used to meet surfers there – "We used to hear how wild they were, but they were always polite and helpful to me. But once your father got ill, I gave it up, of course." Towards Little Waihi, Mum pointed out the bar, where the river met the sea. "We turn here, and walk around the estuary home." Beyond the bar, the estuary formed a long harbour, its waters gently lapping against sand and boat docks.

At home, Dad, now awake and lying on the sofa in the living room, waiting for us, asked me if I'd like a beer. "I always have one at this time of day." I remembered how my old-fashioned father never used to offer any of us girls an alcoholic drink; the first time he offered me one was on my first visit home after I'd married. So now he poured beers for himself and me while Mum made dinner. He told me it was all right if I smoked with my beer. "After all," he said, "I inflicted all that on Jean and you kids for so many years. Mind you, I hate the things now, knowing what they've done to me. But you're your own woman."

"See my scar," he said. He hoisted himself upright and lifted his shirt. "Look, isn't it big, curves all that way round from my front to my back! Christene nearly fainted when I showed her; shouldn't have, I suppose. Didn't know she couldn't stand that sort of thing." He lowered his shirt and said, "They did one of those ultrasounds on me first. I said, what, do you think I'm pregnant? How far along am I? Gosh, they laughed!" And he did now, at the memory of his witticism, and it was his old laugh, his body shaking with wheezing gusts as his laugh rose to a falsetto, to die down in fits of coughing.

Much of our talk concerned his cancer. During the seventies there was controversy around doctors' lack of communication with their patients. I asked him if his surgeon had been communicative with him. "Oh cripes yes," he groaned. "Tells me too much – lots of stuff I don't even want to know about."

When we sat down to dinner, I noticed he ate differently. Farmers build up big appetites, and Dad had been no exception. He always ate heartily, but in the past he had interrupted his eating to sip tea and talk, recount anecdotes from his day and gossip about the neighbours. Now he ate heartily too, but with a silent, snatched greed. He seemed to inhale the food, taking in-breaths before each mouthful as if to vacuum it up, then chewed greedily with his mouth open, his bulging eyes staring down at his plate. It was as if he had to grab this corporeal pleasure or it would be denied him. I was reminded of the time another child gave me a bag of sweets. I wasn't allowed them at home, so knowing they would later be taken from me, I stood on the country road and ate them all, even swallowing some of them whole in my greed to get them into myself before I went home.

The days settled into a pattern. Each morning, the mail was delivered to the stack of communal boxes and several of the retired neighbours gathered around them to collect their mail and pass the time of day. Dad, always enjoying talking to people, what he called "yarning," interested in other people's news and gossip about anyone, made the short walk to the boxes. I recalled how, in our farmhouse, from his seat at the dining table beside the window, he'd watch cars going by on the country road, idenfying the people in them and wondering aloud about their destinations. "That's the McLeods. They must be going into town. They're both wearing suits and Joan's got her best hat on." Then, "They've just driven back the other way! Must've forgotten something." A few minutes later: "Ah, there they go again to town." Then the telephone rang, and because we were on a party line, he could tell by the ring that it was the McLeods' number. He got up, went to the phone, hanging on the wall, and detached the receiver. "If you want the McLeods," he announced into it, "you won't find them home. I've just seen them go by our house in their car. It looks as if they've gone into Whakatane."

When he came home with the mail, he put it down on the kitchen table. Over morning tea, Mum opened all the envelopes, and I noticed that whenever these were letters, she scanned them before reading out the contents. I wondered why, until one day she read that certain grandchildren sent their love and prayers to Grandpa. There was a sudden noise from my father: he put his head down to the table, covering his face with one hand while he pulled a handkerchief from his pocket, and I realized he was crying. He stumbled up from the table and went off to the bedroom. He emerged a short time later, now calm, sat down at the table again, and asked Mum: "What else do they say?"

Mum said to me afterwards, "Oh dear, I shouldn't have read that part. He always cries when they say something like that. He's not used to it. He wants you all to write about what you're doing, and not say anything about his illness. It upsets him otherwise."

He used to scorn those who cried. Even when I was a child, Dad would demand, "What've you been bawling about?" if I appeared with red eyes. I knew of only one other time when he had cried. One of my sisters had converted to Catholicism, and when he told me, he shocked me by bursting into tears and then literally crying on my shoulder. Dad was a Presbyterian, and although he had made us go to Sunday school – we won all the attendance prizes – he never went to church. "Those Catholic priests," he sobbed to me, 'they're laughing at me now. They've got another one, and it's one of my children." He then pulled himself away from me, "Gotta go to the shed," he said, and stumbled away to calm himself with work.

Bewildered and distressed for him, I asked Mum about this grief. She told me she didn't know where it came from, and that he'd even been unable to sleep because of it. He had sometimes mentioned Catholics, including priests, that he knew in his sociable life, but apart from calling Catholics 'tykes" – a common nickname for them then – and immediately assuming that any children called Mary or Joseph must be Catholics, I couldn't recall any resentment or hostility that would have led him to feel this degree of emotion, arising, I felt, from some deep sense of betrayal by my sister.

As she always did when I came home on holiday, Mum said, "You've been working hard. You're just to vegetate." Living in land-bound Edmonton, I was hungry for the sea. So each afternoon, I set out on the walk from the cottage to the ocean, following the path around the end of the estuary, past the bar, and then on to the ocean beach. On my first excursion, I found myself looking at my watch frequently, checking how long I had been there and how much time it would take to walk back to the house. After a few days, I let myself drift in time and space. I took a beach towel and book with me, but when I spread my towel on the sand and settled on it, I mostly didn't read, contenting myself with watching the lines of the breakers, each in turn rearing up to curl over, its underside an intense green, to crash down for its run over the sand, then to draw back into the ocean with a scrape of shells. Or I walked slowly through the thick, white sand along the high tide line, picking up seaweed, driftwood, and shells, then putting them back down again and wandering on.

When I returned it would be late afternoon, and either Dad or I would fetch the beer, and we'd sit and talk while Mum made dinner. One day, he said to me, "You and Kathy are the only ones who still smoke. All the others have given it up."

"And," I teased, "you may as well say it, because you're probably thinking it – Kathy and I are also the only ones who have university degrees, and are the only ones who're divorced!" Dad had always been a domineering father. If we dared stand up for ourselves, we may incur only further scorn and belittlement, but sometimes he was strangely gratified. Now, as he lay back on the sofa, his eyes suddenly got bright with amusement, and he laughed, his whole body shaking with it, until his falsetto broke down into the usual coughing.

He had opposed my desire to go to university. A man who believed that education existed only to inculcate the three Rs, reading, writing, and arithmetic, and who had left school without regret at the earliest possible age, he thought that anything else was a waste of money, both his and what his children could be earning at work. He'd extolled arithmetic especially, and if a girl had to have a job – which she would keep only until she married – her height of ambition should be as a bank teller. Girls on his side of the family had mostly served in shops. Although he was proud of me for always achieving high marks in my best subjects, English, French, and history, he despised those subjects. He also valued sports, in which I didn't do well and took little interest.

When my sister Margaret and I were both in high school, I was a solitary student, achieving my high marks by my own efforts. Margaret's marks were less in spite of being a sociable student, on the phone every night to friends, pooling answers to homework questions. One night she asked me to help her, and, by extension, her friends, with a problem they were having with their French homework. Tired after having spent several hours after school playing the piano for a ballet class, my after-school job, then doing my own homework after dinner and now wanting to spend the short, precious time before bed reading my library book, I refused, telling

154

her they could look it up in their French textbooks. Frustrated, she stamped out of the room.

Dad looked up from an agricultural journal and said to me, "You could have helped her. You're good at French, and you know she isn't."

I put down my book and said, "What she wanted is something simple she should know, and her friends should know. It's right in their French books. They could look it up." And suddenly I shouted: "You've always favoured her!"

He retorted: "And why shouldn't I? She's good at things I value, like sports, and you aren't. You're good at things I couldn't care less about."

When my marks for the nation-wide School Certificate examinations arrived in the mail and I realized I had broken our high school's record for best overall marks, Mum was very happy for me. She said, "You must go over to the shed and show this to your father. He'll be so proud!" Eagerly, I snatched up the piece of paper, ran over to the shed, and gave him the paper. He took it up, read it, and then handed it back to me. "Humph. If you were good at anything decent, I'd be pleased."

He reluctantly let me stay on in school for my matriculation year. Toward the end of that year, when I made it clear that I still wanted to go away to university, he visited his bank manager and brought home coloured pamphlets with titles like "Your Career in Banking." Handing them to me, he said, "You might want to take a look at these" – meaning that he hoped I would stay at home and get a job in the bank. I wasn't proud to remember how I'd barely looked at them, just casting them aside. Yet, when I persisted, and got a government job in Auckland that was full-time but with paid time off for my university lectures, he supported me, grumbling only at my choice of job, "A government pen pusher" – like many farmers, he hated bureaucracy – "and you'll be working for the meanest of employers." He helped me find a boarding place, and told me that if ever I changed my mind and wanted to come home again, I'd always be welcome and he'd never say, "I told you so." When I graduated from university, he had been very proud of me. Margaret had even been made to postpone her wedding because the date she had chosen "was Noeline's graduation and we're going to Auckland for that."

After I moved to Canada, although he'd been against the idea and never believed I'd stay there – "Two winters, and you'll be back" – he'd become proud of having a daughter in Canada. On my first visit back to New Zealand, after he had greeted me at the airport, Dad said, "Guess who I met here? Alfie Breward! He's meeting his son whose been studying in the States. I told him I was meeting you from Canada. You must come and say hello to him. He'll be so pleased." Mr. Breward had been my geography teacher in high school, but whether he would be so pleased to see me, or if he even remembered me, I wasn't sure, but wanting to please Dad and gratify his pride in me, I tottered reluctantly in his wake as he went over to Mr. Breward and his son. They were preparing to leave but that didn't stop Dad, who broke in on them to draw their attention to us. Mr. Breward and his son were gracious.

One day we went out on the estuary in the outboard motor boat, another boat they'd bought when Dad retired to Little Waihi. Mum's childhood holidays had been spent at the seaside, swimming and boating. Dad had some small interest in boats, but his attitude to swimming had always been, "Why swim in cold sea water when you can take a nice warm bath at home?" and when we went to the beach as a family, he'd always spent the time well up from the beach, under the trees, "yarning" with anyone he met there. So Mum, with her background and experience with the surf ski making her an expert on the waters of the estuary and its complicated channels, stood in the bow of the boat, throwing out arms right and left to direct Dad, sitting in the stern at the tiller, steering, while I, the passenger, passively sat on one of the boards in the middle. He seemed to enjoy himself, getting exasperated only when Mum corrected an occasional mistake – "I meant that way, not there!" reminding me of car journeys in Auckland when I was a car passenger with them. Knowing Auckland better and being the better navigator because she used maps, Mum would occasionally say, "Next left" – and, as Dad turned the wheel left, would shout, "No, I meant right!" Dad, with an exasperated sigh and a muttered, "Make up your mind," wrenched the wheel the other way so the car described an S bend.

In his last years of farming, Dad had taken up golf. His cancer had meant the end of this activity, but he still visited the Te Puke golf club now and again to drink beer and "yarn." He took me there, leading me to a table of elderly men sitting around jugs of beer, and introducing me as his "eldest daughter who's visiting from Canada." After their perfunctory polite inquiries about my life in Canada – "Must be cold up there, eh?" – they got back to what they most enjoyed, yarning, anecdotes from previous times. I have inherited Dad's enjoyment of other people's stories, so I listened with relish to the story of the farmer's wife who had run off with the farm worker, and anxious to put as much distance between themselves and the farmer, had not only gone all the way to Australia, but even right out to Perth on the west coast. "What they didn't know," the storyteller told us, "was that the old man had conked out from a heart attack at home when he realized his wife had gone off with the worker. They didn't need to go all the way to Perth, let alone Australia!"

During my visit, Dad picked up the news that neighbours, a married couple Mum and Dad's age, had split up. Ken had moved out, and had, it was said, a "girlfriend" in Rotorua. It was the talk of Little Waihi, Dad said. We met Ken and his girlfriend when we visited friends Mum and Dad had made in Te Puke, the O'Connor family, who owned the fish and chips shop. "Best fish and chips we've ever had," said Dad. "They ask us to come any time and sit with them in the kitchen while we have our fish and chips. Of course we don't like to go as often as they ask because they're running a business and won't let us pay for our meal. I told them you were coming, and they want us to bring you over for a meal."

As soon as we arrived, Mr. and Mrs. O'Connor greeted Mum and Dad with open arms, then me – "We'd heard you were coming, and hoped Mick and Jean would bring you here for a meal." We followed them past the line of waiting customers into the big kitchen at the back. Their two cheerful teenage daughters were bending over the vats of hot fat, aprons wrapped around their school uniforms, lowering fish and chips in baskets into the vats, and lifting them back out to drain. "Janice and Claire, this is Mr. and Mrs. Penny's daughter from Canada," said Mrs. O'Connor, introducing them briefly to me. "Sit down and I'll set the table for you."

We sat, and Mrs. O'Connor poured cups of tea for us. The girls placed plates of fish and chips before us, and we began to eat.

Mr. O'Connor said, "Have you heard about Ken upping and leaving Marigold? They say he has a girlfriend in Rotorua. He said something about popping in tonight. Well – speak of the devil!"

The door to the kitchen had opened, and a couple stood on the threshold. "Ken!" exclaimed Mrs. O'Connor. "You said you may come tonight. And this is?"

"Angela. I'd like you to meet Angela," the man said, his smile both proud and ingratiating, his arm around the shoulders of the woman standing next to him in the doorway.

It must have been in the fifties when I'd last seen peroxided hair in silvery curls cascading to the shoulders, thick, dark, pancake makeup, and eyebrows pencilled in high, thin, black arches. Also, she was wearing a dress of the sort I remembered sewing in the fifties, with a skin-tight bodice and a full tiered skirt, of pink cotton with white lace outlining the tiers, and I could tell she had made it herself because the seams didn't quite meet at the waistline. Beside her, Ken loomed, tall and thin, his long, white, bowed legs prominent because his shorts ended barely halfway down his thighs, and, way below his knobbly knees, he wore navy socks tucked into brown sandals. I could sense Dad's inner glee at the picture they made.

"How nice to meet you, Angela," gracious Mrs. O'Connor said, "And look who've come to see us tonight – Mick and Jean, and their daughter Noeline who's come all the way from Canada. Take a seat at the table and have a cup of tea. Would you like fish and chips?"

Ken looked around at us, and his smile flickered. "No thanks, we just dropped in to say hello on our way to a party."

As soon as we got into the car, Dad started to laugh. "What a floozie! And there was Ken, beaming all over his silly face!" The car shook with his great, falsetto gusts as Mum drove on. "No fool like an old fool!" he wheezed.

Back at home he lay on the sofa, occasionally still, but then rising as his laughter forced his body up. Suddenly he rolled over, and swung his feet on the floor.

"Think I'll go and see Wally and Esther," he said. "Haven't seen them since they came back."

"Oh dear," Mum said when he'd left the house. "Now it'll be all over Little Waihi. But at least he'll enjoy himself." Dad was late coming home that night.

Towards the end of my time with them, Mum was outside, hanging laundry on the clothes line, when Dad returned with the mail. Sitting at the table, without her, he sifted through the envelopes: "A letter," he said of one of them, "with something else in the envelope. Perhaps it's a present," Pushing away the others, he set it in front of him. Given what Mum had said about reading the mail in advance, I was fearful when he opened the envelope. Out fell a folded handkerchief and a note. He said, "Why's she sending me a hankie?" and began reading the note. Suddenly he flung it down and rushed from the room. I heard him sobbing loudly from his and Mum's bedroom. I picked up the letter and read: "Last time you stayed with us, you left this handkerchief behind. I prayed over it, and knew that God intended you to leave it. You should always carry it with you, and every night when you go to bed, tuck it under your pillow and pray."

Mum came into the room. "I heard Mick crying. What on earth upset him so much?" She saw me reading the letter. "Oh dear, I supposed he opened that letter and read it."

"Read it for yourself," I said. "It's a dilly," and handed it to her.

She did, then put the letter down on the table and looked at me. Mum was raised a fundamentalist, but she said, "No wonder he was so upset. I suppose she means well, but a handkerchief – I don't think that's how God works, do you?"

In his grief over my sister's conversion to Catholicism, although so shocking at the time, he had sought comfort and articulated a reason for it. Now his anguish was inconsolable and beyond explanation: it was a wrenching from some much deeper part of himself, so all-encompassing and racking there was no way to articulate or even share it. I felt he was weeping over everything in his life that had disappointed or humiliated him, the betrayals of his children, and his curtailed hopes of which his death so soon after his enjoyable retirement was only the last. I felt that my father hadn't changed at all; rather, in dying, he was some dreadful culmination of himself.

My last weekend was a holiday one, and my brothers and sisters arrived with their spouses and children. Before Mum drove me to the local airport, Dad said, "We must have a photo of Noeline with the children." So we all lined up for him on the lawn, the children sitting on a long bench in front of us adults, standing behind them, while Mum took photos. When she put down the camera and the children ran off shouting, Dad said, "Goodbye Noeline." I had a momentary wish to put my arms around him but I knew that not only would it be a break from family custom but it would upset him in front of family members, so I simply looked at him and said, "Goodbye Dad."

I watched as he went toward the house. As he went in the door, I saw him pull out his handkerchief and drop his face into it as he disappeared inside. Then I said to Mum, "I'll just get my luggage. It's in the living room." One of my brothers offered to fetch it, and I was happy to agree. I didn't want Dad to even hear the sound of my high heels in the house. My baggage in the car, Mum and I left for the airport.

During the months after my visit, I received letters, detailing his progressive deterioration and suffering. "We're so glad," several of them wrote, 'that you saw him when you did." Far way, in Canada, I felt my distance from his and their suffering. They were facing his approach to death; why should I be spared?

In July, I was diagnosed with breast cancer, and underwent a successful mastectomy, with a good prognosis. "I don't think Dad should know," I wrote to Mum, who agreed with me. I couldn't bear inflicting the news of my cancer on him when he was dying of his. And what was my breast cancer, easily diagnosed and operated on, compared to his fatal lung cancer? All I wanted to do was put mine aside and get on with my work. The loss of a breast was nothing compared to the loss of a life.

He died on December 22, a year after he was diagnosed. At the time of his death, children and grandchildren had begun arriving for the Christmas holidays, and after all the excitement he had retired early to bed. When she later went to bed, Mum found he had died, with, she wrote to me, 'such a peaceful look on his face."

When I received the telegram, although the news was expected and even welcome by then, I felt as if I'd been suddenly cut deeply with a sharp knife, some clean amputation like that of my breast. I was about to go to a guest ranch in the foothills of the Rockies for a few days over Christmas. With my large family in New Zealand who would be with Mum, there seemed no point in rearranging my plans to fly to New Zealand for the funeral, and when I discussed this with an older colleague who had been widowed, she advised me to take my holiday. "Visit your mother next year," she said. "That's when she will need you."

In the mountains, away from my work preoccupations, memories of Dad overwhelmed me. Although other guests were people I'd met there before and whose company I enjoyed, I needed solitude, which they understood. So while they went off on organized cross-country skiing excusions, I tramped slowly around the ranch in the snow in a frenzy of memory. True to my statement to my mother that day on the rocks, nine months previously, and to my relief, my memories were all of Dad as I knew him in my childhood and youth, before he became ill. Some were bitter, making me weep; many were sweet, making me laugh. In the freezing air, my hands in bulky mitts not easily able to rummage in my pockets for tissues, tears were inconvenient; laughter was not.

Untitled 3, Roméo Savoie, 2009

Roméo Savoie

Venezia I

at first nothing can be seen
but this mist lifting out of the water
in a cloud
your eyes fixed stubbornly on me in this look
the history of the earth incense colour
in this calmness night the world held within
the boundaries of its silence this other density
words whispered through dusk
the uncertainty the unending absence
on the other side of the water solitary beacons
towers and churches worn down together
green doors of forgotten temples
harsh light white zebra-striped
you watch people walk by
I hold onto nothing but this desire
a burning you stay on the other side
surfaces lean down and bend into the water

Kouchibouguac II

there in the hollow
this torrent, this turn
a stake emerges unpretentiously
a foundation of stone
the breath of she
who in the past would gather
wild berries in this field
daisies and blueberries
all that remains is this uninhabited calm
these fields blanketed by thorns
birds' feathers
and sun-baked seaspray
I drew by hand
the contour of the villages
you in the picture
near the sea, the marshes
your hair in the fall
and the so precious laughter
the wind from the earth
warm like your warm hand
and the scent of wildflowers
in this abandoned place
near the yellowed fields
the mark of man's passage cannot be erased
his hand on the land
or on the tree
or his footprints chasing the hare
or the wake at the far end of the water
leaving indistinct particles
in the sand
commonplace
is a trap to be banned
when hearts are lost
crushing houses
with the smashing of steam shovels
laughing arrogantly into their whiskey
I drew by hand
the contour of the villages
the imaginary houses

the rickety barns
the wharves where small white boats
are made fast
I step over the fences
foundations ripped open
I am under the silence
under the heat of July
under the weight of shame
to believe that scents float away
that sounds fly away
that paths fade away
that the cries of children disappear
that the laughter of girls fall silent
that memory dies
stems from utter stupidity

stones watching

stones little stones as reveries
hiding in crevices or jumping
along long stretches of water
swirling and twisting as smoke
in fields of scarecrows and wind
earth and straw and rusted metal
shaped like warriors or eagles
pouncing watching taking shape
in life's struggle for survival
again and again watching
hiding and watching where
battles are fought and won

the gift

away in the light
of arched reflections
words following words
coming upon me
like wild horses
as men holding on
to nothing but fear
and unlit matches

remember

I remember mostly sexy laughs
ringing thro' telephone static
unpending distances
soft riplings as art
while pushing out of mind
negative words from all over places
words mixed with envy and desires
and theories
those best suited for the sick
no place for beauty
or silent wanderings in
floral gardens and the such
no place like here
in this silent setting
with birds free to jump
from branch to box
to garden stick stuck in soft ground

signs

signs are but signs
trembling in light
like some parts of you
while we linger in closed solitude
wondering about drenched clothes
and white gorillas
it snows still
the plow widens the path
that leads one back to lily pads
and summer delights supposedly
we run in nakedness
thoughts untwinded
falling over arched bodies
blowing dust from underneath
the pillars

Eaton's parking

driving thro' Eaton's parking space
shifting left to miss potholes
and watersplashes from oncoming cars
wishing it was spring
not this false backdrop
skimpy surfaces no flowers
running up escalators
to trunks and suitcases
eating salad and tea
talking into shining eyes
hiding behind folded hands
and effervescent smile
talking about novels
and writing and trips to Europe
talking too much I say
staying back and looking at passing artists
scanning false menus
and upturned cups
energies widespread travelling
all the way from head to foot
from distances missed
in highschool kitchens
dropping each line in unaccustomed
circumstances one thinks of hidden
places and smoke rising from
lost cabins overlooking vast valleys
away from turmoil and unnecessary agitation
stealing kisses behind pots and pans
as if hiding from grace
or societies bad eyes
shifting backwards to cashiers
frail language teasing enjoying humanity
totally for once not concerned
letting things happen with enjoyment

think

some of the things
that people think
are hidden in the realm
of awe
I once thought
of cities near the sea
where ships sail at dawn
bringing all the songs
with them
my heart is silent again
remembering only what comes
to surface
dwelling in you
like one dwells in a house
in total safety
it is sunday after friday
a soft breeze enters the studio open door
making summer beautiful again
making all the wild men
of the crazy cities
hide in the shade of alcoholic dreams
I once remembered to kiss you
after each step that I took
to keep me steady
while falling in the crazy hole
of remembrance

broken boxes

shall I throw stuff in broken boxes
run down streets that have no lights
and call names to the moon
like howling dogs in the fall
how all these things drain me
for no reason while we could
smother our souls in lost places
and maybe finish in peace
with nothing left
but our will to survive
we are our own enemy
we have theories and scandals
and faith and the good word
we think and such is the way
that we choose to go
the wind chooses to belt me
against the walls of fortune
tear down all barriers of hate
and tells me once more
that the one thing
that holds me
is the love I have for you

the crowd

The crowd grimaces and gesticulates
it is a roisterer its animal movement
scrawls abstract stigmata
in the light of strident reflections
our bodies draw near each other intermingle
we are dissolved inside the crowd
penetrated lynched drunk up

we have also said
a body is frail
having known it we would have let our tears flow
rape hurts
it hardens the gaze
every thing is imaginary almost
you take my arms in both hands
you squeeze yourself very hard so you won't be afraid
as for me I pretend

I am behind a mirror
and I watch with precaution
evaluating the unknown from a distance
going around it

the idea of leaving

arriving here in this place
making sure that everything is ready
asking unending questions
imagining no matter what
allowing myself to be stoned by confusion
having certainties
breaking time's censure

I want to tell you the story of my life
or my death

you have passed through the corner of the shadow
of a single footstep
the canoe overturned on the lawn
the charcoal from an old fire
a few objects like bugaboos
our laughs
and other boats hoisting their sails
the idea of running away
while leaving traces of our passage
summer flows through your arms
the sea is greeting the furious gallops
of those traces that we leave behind

the sea is calm this morning
you moved close to the light
and time broke in two

death has left behind it all
the question raised by others we are
bruised by the cycles of our traditions
the crime is hidden behind the mirror
we must not look into it

I have approached silence in a different way
the ordinary is an animal that lashes out
when it is no longer coddled
throwing myself against the beast
watching the intersections of shadows

174

in a copse of shrubs contemplating the incessant
rhythm
of the wave understanding something
that could come from somewhere else
the non-sense the unequal relations

About the Contributors

Anne R. Lévesque's writing has appeared in *The Danforth Review, Room Magazine, The Dalhousie Review* and *The New Quarterly*. In 2009 she published *Motché Perfect,* a collection of found poetry in chiac, an Acadian dialect spoken in Moncton. She makes her home near Inverness on Cape Breton Island, where she misses chiac.

Beth McLaughlin was born in Grand Falls, New Brunswick. She is a retired teacher, active environmentalist, and world traveller. She's written several children's plays for school dramas, as well as several plays for adult theatre. Recently (2008-2010) she's written a series of newspaper articles on Healthy Communities for the *Moncton Times and Transcript*.

Edward Lemond is a retired bookseller and one of the planners for the Northrop Frye Literary Festival, held annually in Moncton, Frye's home town. He has published several poems in *The Antigonish Review* and short stories in various Canadian literary journals. He grew up in Lafayette, Indiana, and came to Canada in 1969. He lived in Halifax before moving to Moncton in 1993. His poetry collection is called *Yesterday I Thought Winter.*

Elaine Amyot was born in Joliette, Quebec and came to New Brunswick in 1968. She is a retired teacher of French Immersion. After finishing her studies in art at the Université de Moncton she has had more than twenty solo exhibitions and numerous group exhibitions. She is a founding member of Galerie Sans Nom and of Galerie 12, both at the Aberdeen Cultural Centre in Moncton. Her life as an artist was featured on the radio show *Trajectoire (SRC.RDI)* in November, 1996. She won third prize for non-fiction in the 2010 Writers's Federation of New Brunswick competition.

Elizabeth Blanchard's short stories have appeared in a number of literary journals including *Lichen Arts & Letters Preview, Windsor Review, Room of One's Own,* and *Dalhousie Review*, and in *Hard Ol' Spot: an Anthology of Atlantic Canadian Fiction*. Her work will also be appearing in an upcoming anthology published by Demeter Press. She won the Writers' Federation of New Brunswick Literary Competition, and is a recipient of a Creation Grant by the New Brunswick Arts Board. She lives in Dieppe, New Brunswick.

Lee D. Thompson was born and raised in Moncton, New Brunswick. His short fiction has appeared in literary journals across Canada and the US, and in the anthologies *Victory Meat: New Fiction from Atlantic Canada*, *The Vagrant Revue of New Fiction, Hard Ol' Spot: An Anthology of Atlantic Canadian Fiction*, and *New Brunswick Short Stories*. His book *S. a novel in [xxx] dreams* was published by Broken Jaw Press in 2007. He is the editor of the fiction journal *Galleon* and has twice been awarded Creation Grants from ARTSNB, as well as a Creation Grant from the Canada Council for the Arts. He is currently executive director of the Writers' Federation of New Brunswick.

Nancy King Schofield grew up in Saint John, N.B., where she was immersed in music until she became a Registered Nurse. She obtained a B.F.A. from Mount Allison University in 1991. She was a founding member of Galerie 12 in the Aberdeen Cultural Center and served on the board of Imago Print Shop. She has had 39 solo exhibitions and over 49 group shows. She has been writing poetry since 1997, often incorporating her text in her visual art. In 2010 she won first place in the poetry competition sponsored by the Writers' Federation of New Brunswick.

Noeline Bridge writes nonfiction and attempts to write novels. Her nonfiction has thrice won first prize in the Writers' Federation of New Brunswick literary competitions. For money and more instant gratification, she indexes books. Her articles on indexing have appeared in professional journals and as chapters in two books. She co-authored *Royals of England: A Guide for Readers, Travelers, and Genealogists*, and, at present, is compiling a book on indexing names, to be published in 2011.

Roméo Savoie was born in Moncton and holds a Master's in Fine Arts, a Bachelor's degree in architecture and a B.A. From 1959 to 1970 he worked as an architect, before turning to painting in the late 60s. Essentially an action painter, Savoie transmits his great energy to his artwork, using themes he has also elaborated in his literary work. He has had numerous solo and group shows, and he has won many awards and prizes, including the Strathbutler award (1998). His literary work includes six collections of poetry. He is a member of the Order of Canada.

Credits / Acknowledgments

Edward Lemond: "Something Happened" appeared in *The Antigonish Review,* Vol 145 (Spring 2006): 125-126.

Elizabeth Blanchard: "Bitch Curve" appeared in *The Dalhousie Review*, Vol 87, No. 2. (Summer 2007): 241-8. "Molded Trophy-Men" was published in *Lichen Arts and Letters Preview*, Vol. 8, No.2 (Fall/Winter 2006): 28-33. Elizabeth Blanchard gratefully acknowledges the support of the New Brunswick Arts Board.

Roméo Savoie: "Venezia I" appeared in *ellipse*, Vol 69 (2003), translated by Jo-Anne Elder. "Kouchibouguac II" appeared in *ellipse*, Vol 69 (2003), translated by Ida Orenbach. "The crowd" appeared in *Unfinished Dreams* (Goose Lane Editions, 1990), translated by Fred Cogswell and Jo-Anne Elder. "The idea of leaving" appeared in *Unfinished Dreams* (Goose Lane Editions, 1990), translated by Fred Cogswell and Jo-Anne Elder.

www.ingramcontent.com/pod-product-compliance
Lightning Source LLC
Chambersburg PA
CBHW050743250626
47155CB00005B/1898